wizoo Guide

Reaktor 3

Len Sasso

Reaktor 3

(:wizoo:)

Imprint

Publisher   Peter Gorges

Author   Len Sasso

© Copyright 2002 by WIZOO GmbH, Bremen, Germany
Printed in Germany
ISBN 3-934903-40-1

Proofreading   Peter Gorges
Layout and typesetting   Uwe Senkler, Hamburg
Cover design   design-box, Ravensburg
Printed by   Quensen + Ourdas, Lamspringe

Welcome!

Welcome to the world of Reaktor. You have just stepped into a vast panorama of synthesis, sampling, sequencing and sound effects. This book will take you on an extensive, guided tour of Reaktor's multifarious landscape and incidentally help you avoid any quicksand that may be lurking about.

Reaktor can be approached in three, equally-legitimate ways:

◆ as an enormous collection of preset instruments (called Ensembles),

◆ as a synth programmer's paradise,

◆ as a construction kit for building arbitrarily complex sound design tools.

Whichever approach you take, you'll find plenty here to keep you supplied with new and exciting sounds for a lifetime (and that's no exageration).

After dispatching the preliminaries of getting Reaktor up and running on your choice of platforms, we'll devote a good deal of time to an in-depth look at some of the Ensembles that come with Reaktor. These have been selected, polished and filled with presets by the folks at Native Instruments to illustrate the very best that Reaktor has to offer.

The factory Ensembles are just the tip of the iceberg, by the way. Reaktor comes with hundreds of building blocks for creating your own Ensembles. In addition, Native Instruments maintains a vast and ever-expanding online library of user-created Ensembles and tools. An occasional visit there will keep you well stocked with new toys.

Our tour of the factory Ensembles will give you all you need, if your inclination is to use Reaktor rather than build stuff with it. (And let's face it, the music has to begin somewhere.) But, if you're an inveterate tinkerer and never satisfied with anything off-the-shelf, it's time to get out your plastic, shirt-pocket protector and continue on to the next sections.

The do-it-yourself sections guide you through the construction of Reaktor Ensembles in the four basic categories: synthesizers, samplers, sequencers and effects processors. The aim here is to introduce you to the building blocks and give you a comfortable start. Where you go from there is up to you, but you'll definitely have the fundamentals necessary for a journey free of meltdowns.

Happy Reakting,

Len Sasso

Table of Contents

1 First Light

In this chapter, we'll explore Reaktor's landscape and discover that the terrain is not as rough as it might, at first, appear. The off-road part of our journey—where things can get a bit bumpy—doesn't begin until Chapter 3 "Building a Synthesizer" on page 77, so for now, just sit back, let us do the driving and enjoy the ride.

Installation

Needless to say, the first thing you have to do is get Reaktor installed. Reaktor's installation procedure is self-guiding and well documented in the manual, so we won't give exhaustive instructions. But, here is a basic look at what gets installed where on the Mac and the PC. Keep in mind that Reaktor can be used as both a stand-alone program and a VST or DXi plug-in. As a plug-in it can be used as an instrument or as an effect (i. e. for processing audio playback from the plug-in host). All the components for all modes of operation are automatically installed.

Installation on the Mac

- A folder named Reaktor 3 is installed in a location of your choice on your hard drive.
- Altivec and non-Altivec versions of the Reaktor stand-alone application are installed in the Reaktor 3 folder. Double-click the appropriate one to start Reaktor.
- Reaktor fonts, ASIO drivers, the factory library of Ensembles, Instruments and Macros, a read-me file and an empty Ensemble named new.ens are also placed in the Reaktor 3 folder.

If you use a utility such as Conflict Catcher to manage your start-up files, you must be sure those extensions are enabled when you want to run Reaktor.

◆ Three extensions are placed in the Extensions folder inside the System folder related to the hardware protection key. These are: USBWibuKeyDriver, WkMAC.lib and WkMacHandle.

◆ If you choose to have the MOTU plug-ins installed, you will find them in the Motu folder inside the Extensions folder.

◆ If you choose to have the DirectConnect plug-ins installed, you will find them inside the DAE folder in the System folder.

◆ If you choose to have the VST plug-ins installed, you will find them in the VST folder of the desired host application. If you want to use Reaktor as a VST plug-in with more than one host, you will need to copy the VST plug-ins into the other host's VST folders.

◆ There may also be some files installed inside a folder named Native Instruments in your Extensions folder.

Installation on the PC

◆ All Reaktor components are installed in the bin whose path is Program Files\Native Instruments\Reaktor 3\bin

◆ The critical files are gends.dll, niasio.dll, reaktor 3.ext and ISSE.dll (if your processor supports ISSE).

◆ The following plug-in files are also in the bin folder: cwdxpx1.dll, ReaktorDXi.dll, Reaktor 3 VST FX.dll, RkExt1.dll, … , RkExt4.dll and RkExtFx1.dll, … , RkExtFx4.dll.

◆ For VST operation, the files Reaktor 3 VST.dll and Reaktor 3 VST FX.dll are installed in the VST folders of the desired host applications. (When you install a new VST host, be sure to copy those two files to the new host's VST folder.)

◆ The hardware protection key files Wibukey.vxd and Wibuke32.cpl are placed in the Windows System folder.

Overview

When you first launch Reaktor you may see Reaktor's default Ensemble or you may see the remnants of whatever you were last doing in Reaktor. To be sure we're all on the same page, start Reaktor and select New from Reaktor's File menu to open the default Ensemble.

▶ In the Preferences section of Reaktor's System menu, there's a checkbox on the Ensemble page labeled "Reload last ensemble at startup". That is a very handy option once you are comfortable with Reaktor, but I recommend you turn it off (uncheck it) while you are learning Reaktor. That way, whenever you start Reaktor you will get the empty, default Ensemble.

You will now have several windows open:

◆ The Ensemble Control Panel window, labeled "Ensemble-Panel".

◆ The Ensemble Structure window, labeled "Ensemble-Structure".

◆ Reaktor's Toolbar, which is divided into two sections: the Ensemble Toolbar on the top and the Instrument Toolbar on the bottom.

◆ You may also see Reaktor's audio file Recorder and Player windows. If these are open, close them for now.

Ensemble? Control Panel? Structure?

Reaktor's organization can be a bit confusing at first, but it's really very simple. At the highest level there is the *Ensemble*. There is always an Ensemble open whenever Reaktor is running. You can think of the Ensemble as your rack—it holds all the gear.

► You can have as many Ensembles as you want (and Reaktor comes with a ton of them), but the important point is that you can only use one at a time.

There are two views of the Ensemble: the Control Panel view and the Structure view. Roughly speaking, the Control Panel is like the front of your rack and the Structure is like the back. The Control Panel of the default Ensemble has just two controls: *Master* (master volume slider) and *Tune* (master tuning knob). The Structure contains the Audio In and Audio Out Modules, which must be present in every Ensemble. The master slider and tuning knob Modules (cabled to the Audio Output Module) are optional, but it's a good idea to keep them there.

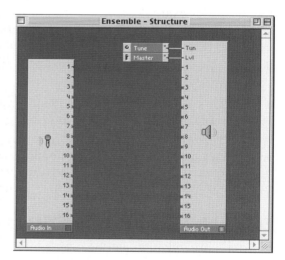

↑ The default Ensemble Control Panel (left) and Structure (right).

As the name implies (and continuing with the rack analogy), Ensembles are collections of things—mostly Reaktor objects called Instruments. Two other kinds of Reaktor objects, Macros and Modules, occasionally appear in Ensembles, but those objects are more typically constituents of Instruments.

In this and the next chapter, we won't be concerned with Structures, Macros or Modules. Instead we will concentrate on Ensembles, Instruments and their Control Panels. These are the operational components of Reaktor—the components you need to understand in order to use the pre-built Ensembles that come with Reaktor. I. e. we're going to play with the gear in the rack, not build it. So, close the Structure window and forget about it for now.

Instruments and their Controls

Although an Instrument can contain as much or as little as its designer wishes, Instruments are typically fully functioning units. For example, a synthesizer, a sampler, a sequencer or an effects unit is likely to be an Instrument. On the other hand, an envelope generator, an LFO, an oscillator or a filter is more likely to be a component in an Instrument rather than an Instrument by itself.

Many Ensembles are made up of a single Instrument. The Ensemble 3-oSC in the factory Ensembles library (see "3-oSC" on page 29) is an example. Others contain several Instruments interconnected in various ways. The Ensemble Fritz FM in the factory Ensembles library (see "Fritz FM" on page 44), for example, contains six Instruments: an FM synthesizer and five effects, each a separate Instrument.

Ensembles and Instruments each have their own Control Panels. Any Instrument control can appear on either Control Panel whereas Ensemble controls (i. e. those not part of an Instrument) can only appear on the Ensemble's Control Panel. That makes it possible to configure more concise Control Panels for an Ensemble containing only the essential controls for the Instruments in the Ensemble, while having the full compliment of controls accessible by opening the Instrument's Control Panel. The Ensemble Cube-X in the factory Ensembles library (see "09 Cube-X" on page 42) is an example of that approach. Only three of the Reverb Instrument's controls are displayed in the Ensemble's Control Panel, while many more controls are available in the Instrument's Control Panel.

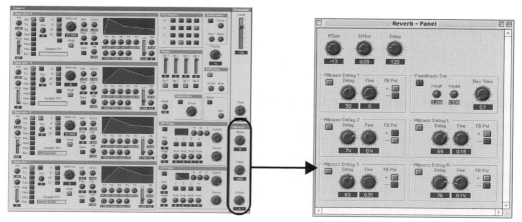

↑ The Cube-X Ensemble's Control Panel (left) with the Reverb Instrument's Control Panel (right).
You can open the Instrument panel by double-clicking on the Instrument's sub-panel in the Ensemble Control Panel.

The Ensemble controls and the controls for each individual Instrument are contained in their own sub-panel within the Ensemble's Control Panel. In the illustration, the Cube-X synthesizer Instrument's controls occupy the sub-panel on the left, the Ensemble controls occupy the sub-panel on the upper-right and the Reverb Instrument's controls occupy the sub-panel on the lower-right.

At any given time, either the Ensemble or one of the Instruments it contains is "blessed" as the focus of attention. In the Ensemble Control Panel, the title bar of that sub-panel is indicated in red (whereas the others are gray). Its name is also displayed in the menu at the far left of the Instrument Toolbar, which is the lower of Reaktor's two Toolbars (see "Reaktor's Toolbars" on page 16). You can also use that menu to make any Instrument or the Ensemble (always the top entry) the focus.

Properties

Each Reaktor object, from individual controls to the entire Ensemble, has its own set of Properties. An object's Properties include aspects of its appearance, how it reacts to MIDI, various aspects of its functioning and descriptive information. The specific Properties change with the type of object.

▶ You can open and edit an object's Properties from the Edit menu, an Instrument Toolbar button or the context menu that pops up when you right-click (ctrl-click on the Mac) the object.

Snapshots

In Reaktor, presets (also known as patches or programs) are called Snapshots. Each Control Panel has its own set of Snapshots, meaning that the Ensemble and each Instrument has its own set of Snapshots. A Snapshot contains the setting of each control in the Control Panel. (Well, there is an exception, but we won't deal with that just now.)

Having separate Snapshots for each Instrument in an Ensemble can lead to lots of confusion, but the Ensemble and Instruments can be set up so that storing and recalling Ensemble Snapshots automatically stores and recalls Snapshot for some or all of the Instruments in the Ensemble. You can set the store-with-Ensemble (called "Store by Parent") and the recall-with-Ensemble (called "Recall by Parent") options in each Instrument's Properties.

You can use MIDI Program Change messages to recall Snapshots, but you can not use MIDI to change banks (i. e. to load a different bank of Snapshots). The Ensemble as well as each Instrument in the Ensemble can have its own MIDI

Channel. If you use the Ensemble's MIDI Channel, any Instruments that have their Recall By Parent property turned on, will have their Snapshots recalled automatically when the Ensemble Snapshot changes.

Reaktor's Toolbars

Reaktor's Toolbar is control central; taking a few minutes now to learn your way around can save you hours of frustration.

The Toolbar is divided into two sections: Ensemble (on the top) and Instrument (on the bottom). The Ensemble Toolbar is used to monitor and control overall Reaktor settings such as the audio sample rate, audio levels and the CPU load on your computer. It also handles file management, MIDI File playback and MIDI remote control. Each of its sections is labeled in the illustration, following which you'll find descriptions of its various controls.

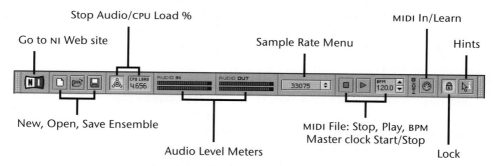

◆ The *NI* button on the left launches your web browser and takes you to Native Instruments' web site. This is an incredible nuisance, especially if MIDI and your Internet connection happen to share the same serial port on your computer. (I. e. click at your own risk.)

◆ The *Save Ensemble* button (floppy disk icon) overwrites the Ensemble file on your hard disk. When you want to save the Ensemble in a separate file, use the Save-As button on the Instrument Toolbar.

◆ The *Stop Audio* button is useful for an overall audio panic. It is also handy for drastically reducing CPU load when you're building Ensembles. I highly recommend turning audio processing off when you load new Ensembles—it can save you from CPU lockups and audio "surprises".

Pressing ⌀ toggles audio processing on and off.

◆ The *Audio Level Meters* indicate the audio input and output levels for the Ensemble.

◆ The *Sample Rate* menu indicates Reaktor's audio sample rate. Everything operates at the same sample rate and you can change it using this menu. (Reaktor has an independent Control Sample Rate that can be set from the Settings menu.

You can often get satisfactory audio results at a greatly reduced CPU load by lowering Reaktor's audio sample rate.

◆ The *Master Clock* buttons start and stop Reaktor's internal Master clock. The Master Clock is used for both synchronization (e. g. of LFOS) and timing of Reaktor sequencers. It also functions as a transport for Reaktor's built-in MIDI File player.

The MIDI File player plays standard MIDI Files, which you can import using Reaktor's File menu. Clicking the Stop button (square icon) twice returns you to the beginning of the MIDI File. Reaktor's Settings menu allows you to toggle MIDI File playback on and off, select whether playback loops and choose whether to ignore tempo changes embedded in the MIDI File.

▶ If you load an Ensemble with a built-in sequencer and nothing happens, that is probably because the sequencer is synchronized to Reaktor's Master Clock. In such cases, you will need to start Reaktor's Master Clock to use the Ensemble. If there is a MIDI file loaded, you can prevent it from playing by turning Play MIDI File off in the Settings menu.

◆ *MIDI Learn* is one of Reaktor's coolest features. It allows you to set up MIDI remote control of any Reaktor Control Panel object on the fly. Simply select the Control Panel object, click the MIDI connector icon and wiggle the desired MIDI Controller. (You can also make these settings in the Properties dialog for the Control Panel object.) The MIDI indicator light next to the MIDI Learn button indicates the presence of incoming MIDI data.

◆ The *Lock* button locks all Control Panel objects in place. The Lock status is saved with the Ensemble and it's a good idea to save them with Lock turned on. That prevents accidentally (and maddeningly) changing a control's position on the panel when you mean to change its value. Turning Lock off is, of course, necessary when setting up a Control Panel.

◆ The *Show Hints* button activates Reaktor's on-screen hints. When turned on, a hint dialog pops up for each control and Reaktor object as the mouse passes over it. Some hints are generic and some are provided by the Ensemble's author. The hints can be very useful when learning a new Ensemble, but they can also get in the way and slow things down when working the Control Panel controls. You can toggle them on and off from your computer keyboard with ⌨ctrl ⌨H (⌘ H on the Mac).

The Instrument Toolbar is used to monitor and control Reaktor settings for the Ensemble or the Instrument indicated in the display at the far left.

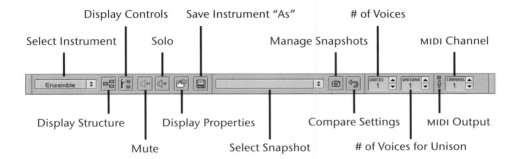

Display Controls   Save Instrument "As"   # of Voices

Select Instrument   Solo   Manage Snapshots   MIDI Channel

Display Structure   Display Properties   Compare Settings   MIDI Output

Mute   Select Snapshot   # of Voices for Unison

◆ The *Select Instrument* menu displays the name object which the Instrument Toolbar currently affects. You can also use it to select the affected object—it lists the Ensemble (always the top entry) and all the Instruments contained in the Ensemble. Another way to select the Ensemble or any Instrument is to make its Control Panel or Structure window active by clicking on it with the mouse.

◆ The *Display Structure* and *Display Controls* buttons open the Structure and Control Panel windows for the selected object.

◆ The *Solo* and *Mute* buttons solo and mute audio from the selected object. They are especially handy when building or auditioning Ensembles with multiple Instruments, in order to hear what each Instrument is doing.

◆ The *Display Properties* button opens the Properties window for the selected Instrument. That is where you set various MIDI and appearance aspects of the Instrument or Ensemble as well as name it and edit the information shown by the hints. Individual Control Panel elements (such as knobs and sliders) also have Properties windows, but the Instrument Toolbar button always opens the Properties window for the Instrument or Ensemble.

◆ The *Save Instrument "As"* button brings up your computer's Save dialog to save the selected Instrument or Ensemble with a new name. It never automatically over-writes a previously saved file.

◆ The *Snapshot* menu lists all the Snapshots for the active Instrument or Ensemble. Generally, recalling and saving Snapshots for the Ensemble will automatically do the same for all Instruments in the Ensemble, but this is an option that can be turned on and off in the Ensemble and Instrument Properties.

◆ The *Manage Snapshots* button (with the camera icon) opens a dialog that allows you to rename, delete and re-place Snapshots.

The first time you click the Compare button after selecting an Instrument, the buffer is empty and all controls will be set to zero.

◆ The *Compare* button is another very handy Reaktor feature, but it takes a little getting used to. Clicking the Compare button swaps the current settings for all controls, with settings saved in a buffer. The first time you change any control's setting after clicking the Compare button, the pre-change settings get placed in the buffer.

You can click the Compare button as often as you like to toggle between two sets of settings. When you decide which you prefer, start making more changes and the preferred settings become the basis for the next comparison.

◆ The *# of Voices* and *# of Voices for Unison* buttons set the maximum number of voices the active Instrument or En-semble can use and when in unison mode, the maximum number of voices that will be used to play a single note. The Processor Usage Limit setting (see Preferences on the System menu) may limit you to fewer voices than the maximum.

◆ The *MIDI Indicator light* flashes to indicate outgoing MIDI messages.

◆ The *MIDI Channel selector* selects the MIDI Channel for the active Instrument or Ensemble. Different Instruments within the same Ensemble can have different MIDI Channels.

Voices, Channels and Outputs

These three concepts—the number of voices, the number of MIDI Channels and the number of audio outputs—are often cause for confusion. A lot of the confusion is caused by the use of the term "mono" in all three contexts. Being clear about how Reaktor deals with these issues is critical, especially when you start building your own Ensembles. Let's deal with voices first.

Each Reaktor Instrument has its own number-of-voices setting, which can be made either in its Properties window or in the Instrument Toolbar. Instrument assigned more than one voice are usually called "polyphonic", whereas those restricted to one voice are called "monophonic" ("mono" for short).

Not to belabor the obvious, but Reaktor carries out separate calculations within an Instrument for each of the Instrument's voices. (If you mouse over a wire when Hints are turned on, Reaktor will show you the value in the wire for each voice.) However, all voices must be combined at the output of the Instrument. In other words, the separate voice calculations are not passed through the Instrument's output.

There is a Module called a Voice Combiner for combining the voices into a single data-stream and it must be used before every output of a polyphonic Instrument. (You can get away without Voice Combiners in a monophonic Instrument, but that's not a good idea because if you later change the Instrument to polyphonic, it will stop working.)

▶ The important thing to remember is that combining the voices at an Instrument's output does not make the Instrument monophonic. It simply combines all the voices into a single audio signal.

▶ Most Reaktor elements have a mono checkbox in their Properties, which when checked, restricts them to monophonic processing. Monophonic Modules, Macros and Instruments have an orange status lamp, whereas polyphonic ones have a yellow status lamp.

Each Reaktor Instrument has its own MIDI Channel assignment and this too can be set in the Instrument's Properties or in the Instrument Toolbar. Assigning Instruments to different MIDI Channels is the way to make an Ensemble multi-timbral—i. e. each MIDI Channel plays a different Instrument with, typically, a different sound.

▶ Keep in mind that whether an Ensemble is multi-timbral has nothing to do with whether it is polyphonic. You could have several monophonic Instruments, several polyphonic Instruments or a combination of both. (For an example, see page 31.)

▶ Another important point is that when using Reaktor as a VST plug-in, whether you can use its multi-timbral capabilities depends on whether your VST host software supports it.

Finally, each Reaktor Instrument can have as many audio outputs as you care to give it. (There can also be as many event outputs as you like, but they don't concern us here.) An Instrument with a single audio output is called "monaural" (again "mono" for short). If there are two outputs, it might be called "binaural" or "stereo", the latter indicating that the outputs are related as with, for example, a synth for which the MIDI Note number controls the panorama position across the stereo field.

If you're using Reaktor as a VST plug-in, the number of audio output channels available to you depends on your VST host software. Most hosts allow at least one stereo output.

As mentioned above, the audio outputs for the Ensemble are managed by the Audio Out Module in the Ensemble Structure. The Audio Out Module can handle up to sixteen audio output channels (not to be confused with MIDI Channels), but the actual number of audio channels available to you will depend on your audio card and drivers.

In summary:

◆ Each Reaktor Instrument has its own polyphony setting and its own audio output configuration.

◆ Polyphonic voices are always combined at an Instrument's output, meaning all individual-voice processing must be done within the Instrument.

- You can achieve multi-timbral operation by using different Instruments assigned to different MIDI Channels.
- You can have up to sixteen independent audio output channels. The actual number depends on your audio card and drivers or in the case of VST plug-in operation, on your VST host.

Audio File Recorder and Player

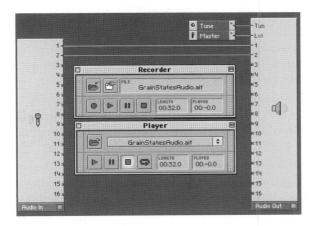

Reaktor's audio file Recorder and Player are used to record and play WAVE and AIFF audio files. The Player sends its playback to Reaktor's Audio In Module for use in any Ensemble. A direct connection to the Audio Out Module (shown here) is the simplest way to audition Reaktor's audio input.

Reaktor has a built-in audio file Recorder and Player. These record and play WAVE or AIFF audio files directly to and from your hard drive. You can open their respective panels from Reaktor's View menu.

The Recorder records Reaktor's audio output just as it appears at the Audio Output Module and the Audio Out meters in the Ensemble Toolbar. When you start Reaktor, the default file name, "untitled Audiofile" will be given to the file and if you've recorded during another Reaktor session using that name, you will be warned about overwriting it. It is a good idea to begin any recording session by first selecting your

own file name and location, which you can do by clicking the File button (red folder icon) at the left of the Recorder.

The Recorder provides a number of options for automating record start and stop. You set these in the window shown left, which you open by clicking the Properties button next to the file folder icon. The options include manual (i. e. clicking the Recorder's transport buttons), MIDI Note events (i. e. Note-On to start and Note-Off to stop) and the Master Clock start and stop buttons in the Ensemble Toolbar. In addition, you can set recording to stop after a certain number of bars. Here are a couple of tips for using the Recorder:

◆ Audio files are always recorded at the sample rate of your audio system, regardless of Reaktor's audio sample rate setting. (The sample rate setting only applies to internal Reaktor processing.)

◆ You can append multiple recordings by using the Recorder's Pause button ⏸. Once you stop recording with the Stop button ⏹, any subsequent recording to the same file name will overwrite the previous recording. (You will be warned.)

◆ You can play back the last recorded file using the Recorder's Play button ▶. If Loop RECORDER Playback is checked in the Recorder's options, playback will automatically loop until you press the Stop button.

▶ If you have the file in the Recorder also selected in the Player, you can not play it from the Recorder.

◆ If you have loaded a file into the Player and have checked Slave PLAYER Controls to Recorder in the Recorder's options, starting the Recorder recording will automatically start the Player playing. This is very handy if you're using the output of the Player in the Ensemble.

Reaktor's Audio Player is for playing WAVE or AIFF files. Its output appears at Reaktor's Audio In Module. This means that if you have nothing connected to the Audio In Module, you won't hear the playback. (You will see it in the Ensemble Toolbar Audio In meters, though.) The purpose of the Player is to use audio files in your Ensembles, but you can also audition its output directly by wiring the Audio In Module directly to the Audio Out Module. As mentioned above, the Player's transport can be slaved to the Recorder's, which is very convenient when recording an Ensemble that uses the Player.

One last thing to mention is that there are also mono and stereo TapeDeck Modules that can be wired directly into your Ensembles for recording and playing audio files either to and from memory (RAM) or disk.

Menus and Key Commands

All of the Toolbar operations can also be carried out using Reaktor's menus. Many of them can also be carried out using context-menus associated with various Reaktor objects and displays and this is often the most convenient way to access those operations. (In some cases, it's the only way.)

Context menus are familiar to Windows users and are always accessed by clicking on the object with the right mouse button (right-clicking). They are less familiar to MacOS users, but are growing in popularity. On the Mac, you access a context menu by holding ctrl while clicking with the left (often the only) mouse button.

▶ If you have a multi-button mouse, it may be set up so that one (or a combination of two) of its buttons automatically does this (i. e. holding ctrl is not necessary). I highly recommend getting a multi-button mouse and setting it up this way.

The use of modifier keys also varies between Windows and MacOS. Windows users have two (ctrl and alt) while MacOS users have three (`ctrl`, `⌥` and `⌘`). Unless otherwise stated, the following relationships are assumed:

◆ `ctrl` for Windows users corresponds to `⌘` for MacOS users.
◆ `alt` for Windows users corresponds to `⌥` for MacOS users.

In the text, I will use the Windows modifiers, only occasionally restating these relationships as a reminder. Similarly, I will refer to right-clicking without mentioning the MacOS alternative.

2 The Factory Library

In this chapter we'll take a look at some of the Ensembles that come on the Reaktor CD. These fall into four broad categories: synthesis, sampling, sequencing and effects processing. Of course, with something as flexible as Reaktor, there's plenty of cross-over, so you'll find some of each category spilling over into the others. You'll find these Ensembles both on the Reaktor CD and in the Factory folder inside the Ensembles folder on the WIZOO CD.

We've chosen Ensembles to illustrate a broad range of Reaktor's features. Each is accompanied by a large assortment of Snapshots and many also come with a MIDI file to illustrate their range of sounds. The MIDI files are in the same folders as the Ensembles and have the same names except for the extension (.mid instead of .ens). If you have not changed their name or location, the MIDI file will load automatically with its Ensemble.

I strongly recommend that you read this chapter at your computer with Reaktor running. Here are the steps I suggest:

1   Load the relevant Ensemble. Ensure the Ensemble Control Panel is open and that all other Control Panel and Structure windows are closed.

2   On the Settings menu, make sure that "Play MIDI File" is turned on (checked), that "Loop MIDI File" is turned off and that "Ignore Tempo Changes" is also turned off.

3   Start the MIDI file playing by clicking the Master Clock's Play button in the Ensemble Toolbar (see "Reaktor's Toolbars" on page 16). Remember you can completely rewind the MIDI file by clicking the Stop button twice. It remains indented to indicate that the file is at the beginning.

4   As you listen to the MIDI file playback, notice the Snapshot changes in the Instrument Toolbar and watch for real-time automation in the Control Panel.

5   Read the Ensemble description in this chapter, playing around with the various controls and Snapshots as you go.

▶ On the Mac, you can change Snapshots from your computer keyboard by typing ⊞ and ⊟. On the PC, you can do this by typing ⬆ and ⬇, but only if the Snapshot menu is selected.

▶ On all platforms, you can use the computer keyboard to play notes in Reaktor. The key assignments mimic a piano keyboard with C on ⍾ and Ⓠ, C# on Ⓢ and ②, ..., B on Ⓜ and Ⓤ. ⬆ raises all keys two octaves and ctrl⬆ lowers all keys two octaves.

Finally, if you have a MIDI control surface, I suggest you make use of Reaktor's MIDI Learn function on the Ensemble Toolbar (see "Reaktor's Toolbars" on page 16) to MIDI remote some of the controls. If your control surface features incremental controls (i. e. continuously rotating knobs) as does Native Instruments' 4Control, you will find MIDI remote control even more useful. There's nothing like a little tactile feedback when tweaking a synth's parameters.

▶ You can also use the computer keyboard to change the value of the selected Control Panel control. ⬆⬇ increment and decrement the value by the control's step size. On the PC, the Page Up/Down keys increment and decrement by ten times the step size.

Synthesis

In this section, we'll start off with several classic subtractive synthesizers, then move on to FM and hybrid models that employ other synthesis methods. Several of the Ensembles in this section are modeled after classic hardware synthesizers. We won't attempt to judge how close a match they are sonically, but guarantee they will give you that "vintage" experience.

Subtractive synthesizers start with oscillators and perhaps a noise generator, then use filters to alter the harmonic content of the sound. (That is called "subtractive synthesis" be-

cause in the simplest case, filters reduce harmonic levels—
i. e. subtract from the harmonic content. However, resonant
filters can also boost harmonics and may even create them
by self-oscillation and distortion.)

The two other common elements of a subtractive synthesizer are envelope generators (envelopes, for short) and low
frequency oscillators (LFOS). Envelopes are typically applied
to filters to contour the filter's effect. They are also applied to
the overall output level of the synthesizer. LFOS are typically
applied to pitch and output level to produce vibrato and
tremolo.

Ok, that's the simplest case. In reality, all of these classic
synth elements can be used, abused, modified and expanded
in numerous ways, as you'll discover with the synthesizers
covered in this section.

3-oSC

Instrument   NI
Sounds   Sound Burst
Demo   M. S. Zanx

◎ **02** oSC

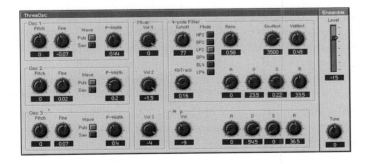

The Ensemble Control
Panel for 3-oSC—a
generic subtractive
synth model.

3-oSC is a standard subtractive synthesizer in the classical
style. It features three oscillators (surprise) with sawtooth or
variable-width pulse waveforms. The oscillators are mixed
and sent to a multi-mode, resonant filter. The filter features
keyboard tracking and a standard ADSR (Attack, Sustain, De-

cay and Release) envelope for the filter cutoff frequency. The final stage is an amplifier with its own ADSR envelope. Can't get much more straightforward than that, right?

Because the 3-oSC Ensemble contains a single Instrument, the Ensemble has no Snapshots. Selecting the Instrument in the Ensemble Control Panel or the Instrument Toolbar's Instrument menu will make the 3-oSC Instrument's Snapshots available.

If you've been wondering how the pros got so much mileage out of their Arp Odysseys, Minimoogs and Oberheims in the early days of portable synths, a little time spent with 3-oSC will reveal their secrets.

Here's a trick that is not strictly in keeping with our agreement not to talk Structure in this section. Since 3-oSC is not a CPU hog, you can easily upgrade it to a multi-timbral version by duplicating the 3-oSC Instrument and assigning the copies to different MIDI Channels. You'll also need a little mixer and with four of these things, you may need to reduce Reaktor's audio sample rate (think of it as retro).

You'll find the Ensemble pictured here in the WIZOO Ensembles folder under the name "3-oSCx4". The 3-oSC Instruments are assigned to MIDI Channels one through four and they have been given different voice allocations appropriate to their intended function: Lead (1 voice), Bass (1 voice), Poly (8 voices) and Pad (4 voices).

The four channel mixer on the left both stereoizes the output allowing each mono 3-oSC to be panned and provides on/off buttons for each 3-oSC. (You'll find a Macro version in the Macros folder on the WIZOO CD.) The on/off buttons are important because when a 3-oSC module is turned off, it is removed from the audio signal path and does not drain CPU cycles.

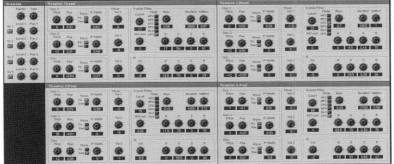

Multi-Timbral upgrade for your 3-oSC synth.

Junatik

Instrument   NI
Sounds   Easy Sounds, Joerg Holzamer, ear2ear, Uwe G. Hoenig
Demo   Joerg Holzamer

◎ **03**   Junatik

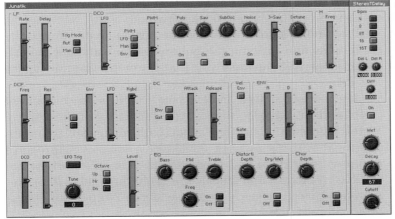

The Ensemble Control Panel for Junatik—an emulation of the famous Roland Juno series of synthesizers from the mid 80's.

The Juno series of synthesizers from Roland was one of the most popular product lines of the mid 80's. The first in the series, Juno-6, was introduced in 1982 followed soon after by the Juno 60, which added MIDI control and patch memory.

The final and probably most popular synth in the series was the Juno 106, used extensively by, among others, Duran Duran and Vince Clarke.

Junatik is a Juno emulation with some 21st century additions including EQ, chorus, distortion and a tempo-sync'd stereo delay. Its oscillator section is also beefed up with a detunable "3-saw" oscillator.

Structurally, Junatik contains two Instruments, the synth emulation named "Junatik" and the stereo delay named "StereoTDelay". If you played the MIDI file, you may have noticed that only the Junatik Instrument's Snapshots change. (StereoTDelay Snapshot 11 is recalled once at the beginning.) That is because the Instruments and the Ensemble are all assigned to different MIDI Channels in their Properties window (see "Properties" on page 15).

Junatik's oscillators are located in the top-middle of the Junatik control panel, in the section labeled "DCO". There are actually four oscillators (variable pulse, sawtooth, square-wave sub-oscillator and triple sawtooth with detuning) as well as a noise source. Each can be turned on or off with the *On* buttons and toggling the buttons while watching the CPU LOAD meter will convince you that fewer oscillators require less CPU.

The DCO is followed by a 4-pole (24dB/octave) resonant lowpass filter, labeled "DCF" at the left-center of the Control Panel. The remainder of the signal path consists of an amplifier (DCA) with its own AR envelope, a shallow 6dB/octave highpass filter (HPF) and three effects: 3-band EQ, distortion (a clipping circuit) and chorus (an LFO'd dual delay-line). Remember, there is also the separate stereo 2-tap delay Instrument, StereoTDelay.

In addition to the AR envelope generator built into the amplifier, there is an ADSR envelope generator (ENV) that can be applied to the amp (instead of the AR envelope), to the filter cutoff with positive or negative polarity and to the pulse-width. The LFO (top-left) can be applied to the same three destinations as well as to pitch. The LFO has its own fade-in envelope that can be triggered either manually (using the LFO Trig button) or by each MIDI Note. The Delay slider sets the attack time and the release time is fixed at zero. (Pulse-width modulation is always via the un-delayed LFO.) Velocity can be routed to envelope and gate amounts using buttons in the VEL section of the Control Panel.

Conventional wisdom has it that the heart of any subtractive synth is in its filter. Junatik's resonant lowpass filter is actually a rather complex construction designed to emulate the Juno filters. It consists of two 2-pole filters in series, a soft-saturation feedback circuit and a non-linear resonance control. We've performed a little open-heart surgery and inserted two other Reaktor filters, the Pro-52 filter emulating the filter on the Sequential Prophet 5 and the Ladder filter emulating the Minimoog 4-pole lowpass filter. The Mode switch allows you to switch between filters—you'll hear quite a difference on most of the Snapshots. The meter beside the Res slider illustrates its non-linearity; notice that the meter does not rise in sync with the slider. You'll find the Junatik+ Ensemble in the WIZOO Ensembles folder.

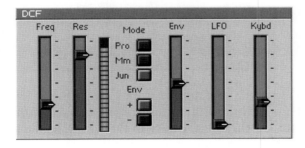

Junatik's DCF module as modified in the Ensemble, Junatik+. The resonance meter exposes the Res control's non-linearity. The Mode switch switches between the Junatik, Minimoog and Prophet filters.

To get a feel for the many sounds possible with Junatik or Junatik+, I recommend playing a small, looping MIDI file with the StereoTDelay turned off while stepping through the Junatik Snapshots. You'll find an eight bar loop, JunatikLoop.mid, extracted from the Junatik MIDI demo file in the WIZOO MIDI Files folder.

ManyMood

04 ManyMood

Instrument   NI, Easy Sounds
Sounds   Easy Sounds
Demo   M. S. Zanx

The Ensemble Control Panel for Many-Mood—an emulation of the famous Minimoog.

ManyMood is the Premium Library's salute to the Minimoog. I won't insult you with a description of the Minimoog—if you've never heard of it, you're in the wrong business.

ManyMood starts out with the standard Minimoog compliment of sound sources: three multi-waveform oscillators (with a few more waveforms than the original), a white/pink noise generator and an external audio input. These are mixed and passed through an emulation of the classic Moog-style resonant, 4-pole lowpass filter. (This emulation, created in an earlier version of Reaktor, is constructed by using two 2-pole filters in series with a clipping circuit between. Reaktor 3 contains a single filter Module to emulate the Moog filter.) There are separate ADSR envelopes for amplitude and filter cutoff. In the original Minimoog, Oscillator 3 could function as an LFO. In ManyMood, both Oscillators 1 and 3 have this feature.

ManyMood adds some features not found on the Minimoog. For one thing there is velocity control for both filter and amplifier envelope amounts. (Of course, the Minimoog did not have a velocity sensitive keyboard—you were lucky that there was a keyboard at all in those days.) In addition, there is a Cross Modulation circuit, which multiples the output of Oscillators 1 and 2. Cross Modulation produces effects similar to Ring Modulation and has the most noticeable effect when Oscillator 2 is detuned.

ManyMood adds an assortment of effects to the basic Minimoog design. These include 4-band EQ, clipping distortion, ring modulation, chorus, reverb and stereo delay with normal and crossed feedback. You'll notice two additional Instruments in the Ensemble Control Panel labeled InputDiff and Reverb. If you happen to nose around in the Ensemble Structure you won't find these Instruments. That is an artifact of the designer's choice to include these Instruments inside the Reverb Macro in the ManyMood Instrument. (If that mouthful alarms you, just ignore it.) That allows him to include a minimal set of Reverb controls in the Ensemble panel while still giving access to the full compliment of Reverb and Input Diffuser controls by double-clicking their respective Control Panels in the Ensemble Control Panel.

ManyMood's effects, while a welcome enhancement, can get in the way of the classic Minimoog experience. In the WIZOO Ensembles folder, you'll find an Ensemble named "ManyMood+" with an added switch in the bottom-center of the Control Panel for turning all the effects off at once. (Recalling Snapshots for that ManyMood Instrument in that Ensemble has no effect on this switch.) Try the ManyMood demo MIDI file with the ManyMood+ effects turned off.

Me2SalEm

Instrument   Josue Arias, NI, John Bowen
Sounds   John Bowen
Demo   NI

The Ensemble Control Panel for Me2SalEm— an emulation of the classic Oberheim two-voice.

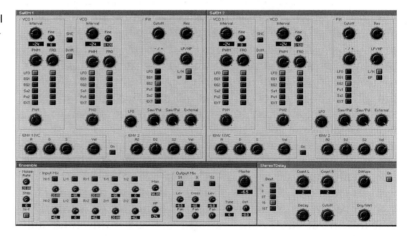

Me2SalEm is a loose emulation of the Oberheim 2-Voice synthesizer. The Oberheim synthesizers of the mid 1970's were all based around the two oscillator Synthesizer Expander Module (SEM for short). The SEM oscillators offered sawtooth and variable-width pulse waveforms. The filter was a resonant, 2-pole, multi-mode (lowpass, highpass, bandpass and notch). There were two ADS envelope generators and an LFO. Most 2-Voices also had an eight step analog sequencer with a noise source and sample-and-hold circuit built in.

One unique feature of the SEM was the availability of patch points (via Molex connectors on the module's circuit board) for most of the control voltage sources and destinations. With a drill, a soldering iron and a high risk-tolerance, you could turn an SEM into a patchable modular synth.

Me2SalEm expands on this theme by adding a few switch matrices to the SEM front panel and providing a flexible audio mixer/router. You'll also find the StereoTDelay familiar from the Junatik Ensemble. Sadly, the little analog sequencer is missing, however we've remedied that in the Ensemble, Me2SalEm+, which you'll find in the WIZOO Ensembles folder. You'll also find a mini-sequencer Instrument in the Instruments folder on the WIZOO CD under the name "Obie Stepper".

Me2SalEm Mini Sequencer

Me2SalEm's signal path is potentially quite complex and deserves a little explaining. Each SEM has three potential audio sources: VCO 1, VCO 2 and EXT. These are mixed with the knobs at the bottom of the Filt section. The two *Saw/Puls* knobs control the VCO inputs to the Filter—they are bi-polar: left of center for sawtooth, center for no input and right of center for pulse-wave input. (See "BiPolar Knob" on page 206.) The *External* knob is a standard level control for the external input.

The output from each SEM is sent to the Output Mixer whose Control Panel is at the right end of the Ensemble section of the Control Panel. The Output Mixer also contains a multiplier for the two SEM outputs which works similarly to the Cross Modulation section of ManyMood. The Output Mixer contains switches, level and pan controls for each SEM and the cross mix.

The Input Mixer (also in the Ensemble section of the Control Panel) controls the audio signal appearing at the Ext input of each SEM. Sources include noise from the little noise generator at the left, Reaktor's left and right external audio inputs and the output of each SEM (i. e. each SEM can be an external input to itself or the other SEM). There are switches and level controls for each of these possible sources. The Input Mixer also contains a 1-pole highpass filter whose cutoff frequency is set by the HP control and a clipping circuit whose clipping levels are set by the Max control.

The SEMs themselves are fairly straightforward. Either VCO can have its frequency and pulse width modulated by the LFO, either envelope generator, the saw or pulse output of the other VCO or the EXT input. The Filter has the same modulation sources as the VCOs—the modulation amount and polarity are controlled by the +/– knob. The Filter is 2-pole resonant with highpass, bandpass and lowpass outputs. The highpass and lowpass outputs can be mixed using the *LP/HP* knob or the bandpass output can be used.

SH-2K

◎ **06** SH-2K

Instrument   NI, Easy Sounds
Sounds   Easy Sounds
Demo   Easy Sounds, NI

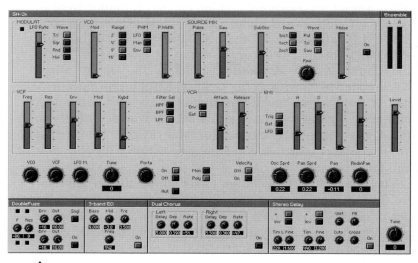

↑ The Ensemble Control Panel for SH-2k—an emulation of the Roland SH-101 bass synth popular for drum & bass, techno and acid tracks.

The Roland SH-101 is a monophonic bass synth with built-in arpeggiator and sequencer. It was first produced in 1983 and was an instant hit. There was no patch memory or MIDI although after-market MIDI retrofits became quickly available.

The Reaktor implementation is, of course, not monophonic, has MIDI and patch memory and has the add on effects you're no doubt familiar with by now: distortion (called DoubleFuzz), EQ, chorus and stereo delay. No sequencer or arpeggiator, but you can get some interesting motion by using the LFO to trigger the ADSR envelope.

SH-2k starts with a noise generator and three oscillators: variable-width pulse wave, sawtooth and detunable multi-wave. These are mixed in the SOURCE MIX section (top-right) and sent to the filter section, labeled VCF. The filter is actually two 2-pole filters in series. The first filter is switchable between lowpass, bandpass and highpass modes, whereas the second is always lowpass. The filters' cutoff frequencies and resonance amounts are linked. The amplifier, labeled VCA, has a dedicated AR envelope, but can also be controlled by the ADSR envelope. The ADSR envelope can be applied to the filter cutoff and the oscillator pulse-width.

The LFO has triangle, square, random and noise outputs. It can be used to modulate pitch, pulse-width and filter cutoff. It can also be used to trigger the ADSR envelope. When the VCA is controlled by this envelope, you can use it to get sequencer-like effects.

SoundForumSynth

Instrument   Stephan Schmitt, NI
Sounds   Peter Gorges

The Ensemble Control Panel for the Sound-Forum synth—a synthesis tutorial with a little bit of every-thing.

The SoundForum Ensemble was specifically designed by Native Instruments for Peter Gorges's Sound Forum column appearing in the German and American Keyboards magazines. Since the column covers all aspects of basic synthesis, the SoundForum Ensemble has a little bit of everything, including an oscilloscope (far right) to show you what's going on. Step through its well thought out Snapshots for a quick tutorial on basic synthesis.

Uranus

Instrument   Olivier Gerber
Sounds   Olivier Gerber
Demo   M. S. Zanx

⊚ 08   Uranus

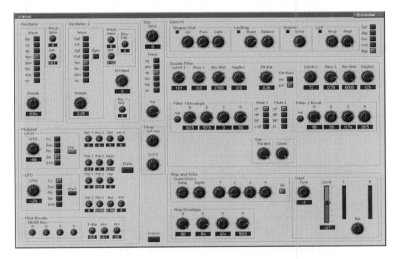

The Ensemble Control Panel for Uranus—the most extensive and expensive of the factory library subtractive synths.

Uranus is the most complex as well as the most CPU consuming of the subtractive synths. It is especially well suited for pads (listen to the demo MIDI file), but don't overlook its potential for basses, leads and effects.

One thing that makes Uranus such an effective pad synth is its Quad Chorus, which uses four delay lines and is responsible for about 20% of Uranus' CPU load. You can turn it off for more voices, but better yet, leave it on and live with fewer voices or a lower sample rate.

Uranus has a lot of everything: three multi-waveform oscillators, two multi-mode filters, four ADSR envelope generators and two multi-waveform LFOs. Virtually any modulation routing you can imagine is provided and in a nice touch, you can freeze the LFOs using the Static button. By default, this is assigned to MIDI Controller 66 (Sostenuto Pedal) and can be used to great effect when playing Uranus live.

Aside from the Quad Chorus, there are four distortion effects (top-right): two wave shapers, a wavewrapper and overdrive. You can only use one of these at a time, but one is definitely enough.

Cube-X

09   Cube-X

Instrument   SolarX, Jörg Holzammer, NI
Sounds   Jörg Holzammer, SolarX
Demo   Jörg Holzammer

The Ensemble Control Panel for Cube-X—featuring four multi-waveform FM operators and a full compliment of effects.

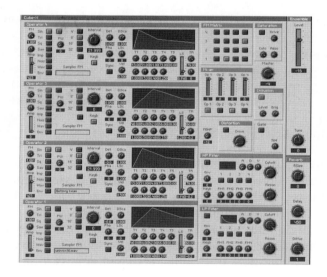

Cube-X is a complex hybrid based loosely on the FM model. Owing to its variety of oscillator types (including sample playback) it can achieve a range of sounds beyond those possible with classical FM synths using only sine wave oscillators. As one example, listen to the "Loop Trick" Snapshots (27 through 32) that use FM techniques to manipulate a beat loop.

Cube-X has four oscillators (called Operators), any of which can be assigned to modulate any of the others including itself. Each Operator has a six stage breakpoint envelope controlling its output level. The output of the four Operators is mixed and passed through distortion, high and lowpass filters, saturation, reverb and gating sections. As with Many-Mood in the previous section, the effects can sometimes obscure the FM part of the sound. There is a modified version, Cube-X+, in the WIZOO Ensembles folder with a global effects switch (labeled EFX). The EFX switch setting is not affected by Snapshot recall.

The key to understanding what's going on in Cube-X is to first examine the FM Matrix and Mixer sections in the upper-right part of the Control Panel. Each row of the FM Matrix represents an FM destination (i. e. what modulation is being applied to the Operator indicated by the number on the left). Each column of the FM Matrix represents an FM source. In the illustration, Operator 2 is modulating Operator 1 and Operator 4 is modulating Operator 3. The Mixer controls how the Operators are mixed in Cube-X's audio output. In the illustration, Operators 1 and 3 are in the mix while Operators 2 and 4 (the modulators) are muted.

Once you know the players and their positions, move to the Operator controls on the left to see what they're contributing. The FM amount and polarity are controlled by the knobs at the top-left of each operator. The Amp slider controls the output level of the operator when the Operator is used as a modulator—it does not affect the level of the Operator in the mix.

The eight buttons to the right of the level controls determine the Operator's sound source. The top five buttons select different oscillator waveforms. (The button to the right of the *Sin* button substitutes a parabolic waveform for a sine. You'll find this in many FM synths because it produces nearly as pure a tone as a sine wave at significantly less CPU cost.) The bottom three buttons select noise, the FM sample player and the Operator's envelope output. The envelope output is useful as a source when you want to control another Operator's pitch with an envelope.

The remaining controls are for the Operator's pitch, pitch and envelope scaling and envelope breakpoint settings (time and level). The *Keyb* button toggles MIDI keyboard tracking and the *Sync* button syncs the oscillators to MIDI gate events (not to be confused with the more common hard-sync between oscillators). The unlabeled button below the 32' range button locks the Operator's pitch at zero. This is useful when the Operator is used as an FM carrier because it results in only the sidebands being audible.

The Cube-X effects are standard filters, distortion and reverb. Both the lowpass and highpass filter can have their cutoff frequency modulated by any Operator and this is controlled independently by the knobs in the filter's Control Panel. As with ManyMood, the reverb is actually an Instrument embedded inside the Cube-X Instrument, which allows a more complete set of reverb controls to be accessed by clicking the Reverb Control Panel in the Ensemble.

Fritz FM

10 Fritz FM

Instrument   Fritz Hildebrandt
Sounds   Fritz Hildebrandt
Demo   M. S. Zanx

Fritz FM adheres the most closely to the classic FM synth architecture introduced by Yamaha in the DX-7. For standard FM keyboards, leads and pads, this is the one to choose.

Fritz FM offers six Operators with sine or parabolic oscillators. Each Operator has five output buttons (along the right) for routing its output as an FM modulator to any of the other Operators. There is also a switchable audio output which is summed with the audio outputs of the other Operators. Like classic FM synths, Fritz FM has no filter section. It does have a single LFO whose output can be routed to any of the Operators.

The Ensemble Control Panel for Fritz FM— featuring six sine wave operators with overdrive, chorus, phasing, Leslie and tap-delay effects.

Each Operator has a five stage envelope (attack, decay 1, decay 2, sustain and release) for controlling its level at all outputs. There is both keyboard and velocity scaling of the envelope amount and the keyboard scaling can be positive or negative with a breakpoint. That is typical of FM synths and is very useful for Operators used as modulators; it allows you to scale the modulation amount up over the lower keyboard register then scale it down over the upper register where large amounts of FM can cause shrillness and aliasing.

Fritz FM's effects routing is more flexible than the usual series arrangement. The first effect in the chain is an overdrive/distortion unit. That is followed by phaser, chorus and Leslie simulations in parallel. The mix of those four effects is fed to a dual delay line with cross feedback. The Ensemble Control Panel's on/off buttons allow any of the effects to be bypassed. One thing to keep in mind is that the effects don't come cheap. Using them all increases CPU usage by roughly 65%. The most expensive are the phaser and Leslie simulation, adding roughly 20% each to CPU drain.

InHumanLogic

Instrument   InHumanLogic
Sounds   InHumanLogic
Demo   InHumanLogic, NI

The Ensemble Control Panel for InHuman-Logic—featuring six operators, a flexible modulation matrix and multi-mode filtering.

InHumanLogic also adheres closely to the classic FM model, but offers somewhat more complex modulation routings. It is especially well suited to complex, evolving, enharmonic sound effects.

Like Fritz FM, InHumanLogic has six Operators. All have sine and parabolic wave oscillators and two (Operators 5 and 6) also have a variable-width pulse-wave oscillator. The signal path ends in a 4-pole, resonant, multi-mode filter followed by the, now familiar, StereoTDelay. The filter has no envelope, but can be modulated by either of two multi-waveform LFOs. The LFOs can also modulate the Operator pitches and LFO 2 can modulate LFO 1's rate. For a hint at the power of the LFOs, try Instrument Snapshot 2 "Walking at Dark".

The most unique feature of InHumanLogic is its modulation and output routing matrix. The left six columns determine the FM sources for modulation of the Operators corresponding to the numbers along the top. The last three columns control the audio output.

Note that many of the button labels include arithmetic operations. For example, Operator 1 can be modulated by the sum of Operators 2 and 3, the sum of Operators 2 and 4 or the result of dividing Operator 1 by Operator 2. Taking the sum of two signals is similar to mixing them, but multiplying or dividing them generates sidebands, an effect similar to ring modulation. As listening to the Snapshot or demo MIDI file will convince you, that can lead to some complex and interesting sound effects.

Matrix Modular

Instrument   laZyfiSh
Sounds   laZyfiSh

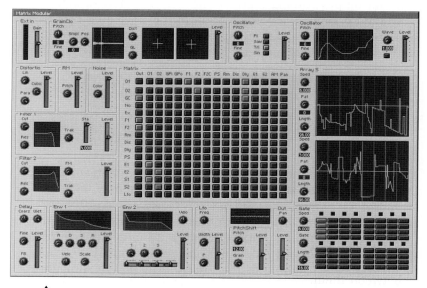

⬆ The Ensemble Control Panel for Matrix Modular—a Hybrid synth/
sampler with a modulation matrix allowing just about anything to modulate anything else. There is a built-in multi-gate step sequencer at the
lower right.

As its name implies, Matrix Modular is a full blown modular
synth that uses a switching matrix (instead of patch cords)
for connecting its modules together. Flexibility is both its
greatest strength and greatest weakness—you can get almost
any sound out of Matrix Modular, but getting there may in-
volve some heavy weather.

As sound sources, Matrix Modular has a one of just about
everything Reaktor has to offer. Here's the run down starting
at the top-left of the Control Panel and moving clockwise:

◆ Ext in: for processing external audio input from Reaktor's Audio In Module. (Tip: You could wire a mono Tape Deck Module into the Matrix Modular Instrument's Ext input to playback a sound file instead of using an external audio signal.)

◆ Grain Cloud: for granular resynthesis of multi-samples with independent control of pitch, grain size and grain spacing.

◆ Oscillator 1: a multi-mode oscillator with square, saw-tooth, triangle and sine waveforms.

◆ Oscillator 2: a wavetable oscillator allowing you to draw your own waveforms.

◆ Noise: a variable-color noise generator.

Audio processing effects include:

◆ Filter 1: a resonant, Moog style Ladder filter. This is a multi-mode filter with outputs for one, two, three and four poles. The raw signal and each of the outputs are wired into a Scanner Module and the *Stage* control crossfades between them. (The Ensemble, Matrix Modular 2+, adds LFO control of the *Stage* crossfade.)

◆ Filter 2: a multi-mode, two pole filter with saturation and FM style cutoff modulation.

◆ Distortion: using a cubic wave-shaper followed by satura-tion.

◆ RM: ring modulation by a built-in parabolic oscillator.

◆ Delay: feedback delay line.

◆ PitchShift: pitch shifting using a granular delay line.

Control sources include:

◆ Env 1: a velocity sensitive ADSR envelope.

◆ Env 2: a velocity sensitive breakpoint envelope. The knobs set the first, second and sustain levels. The horizontal sliders set the times to reach the first, second and sustain levels as well as the release time.

▶ Note that both envelopes are flow-through—they control the amplitude of audio signals routed through them using the Matrix buttons. Both envelopes are automatically gated by incoming MIDI Note messages and the top two tracks of the Gate sequencer.

◆ Lfo: a sine wave LFO with symmetry (*Width* knob) and phase control. Changing the symmetry skews the waveform from ramp-up through sine wave to ramp-down.

◆ ArraySeq: two Event Table sequencers holding 128-event sequences each. You can draw in the sequences using the mouse and use the Event window's context menu to manipulate them.

◆ Gate: four Gate sequencers hard-wired to the two envelopes, sample position reset for Grain Cloud and LFO waveform reset.

Matrix Modular's modulation Matrix is responsible for all modulation and signal routing. Each button has a hint describing its action (when hints are turned on).

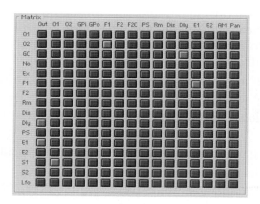

All audio and most control routings are set up using the Matrix section of Matrix Modular. The row labels along the left edge indicate the modulation source, and the column labels along the top indicate the modulation destination. All sources are audio except the bottom three: the pitch sequencer out-

puts S1 and S2 and the LFO output. The first column determines what reaches the final output (and is displayed in the
little oscilloscope above the PitchShift section). The *F1*, *F2*,
PS, *Rm*, *Dis*, *Dly*, *E1* and *E2* destinations represent the audio
signal path. The rest of the destinations are for modulation.
For example, *F2* is the input to Filter 2 whereas *F2C* is for
modulating the Filter 2 cutoff.

The signal path in the illustration uses two sources: Grain
Cloud (*GC*) and Oscillator 2 (*O2*). The output of Grain Cloud is
patched into the Delay (*Dly*) which is, in turn, patched to the
output. The output of Oscillator 2 is patched into Filter 1 (*F1*),
then into Envelope 1 (*E1*) and finally, to the output. Oscillator
1's pitch is controlled by the top pitch sequencer in ArraySeq
(*S1*). Recall that Envelope 1 is automatically triggered by
both incoming MIDI Notes and the top track of the Gate sequencer.

NanoWave

Instrument   Uwe G. Hoenig
Sounds   Sound Burst
Demo   Sound Burst

◎ **13**   NanoWave

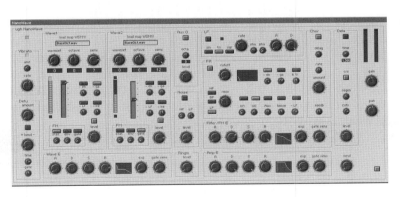

The Ensemble Control
Panel for NanoWave—
a waveset synthesizer
featuring FM, RM and
multi-mode filtering.

NanoWave is a waveset synth reminiscent of the PPG and
Waldorf synths. Its sound sources are two waveset players
(each of which can frequency modulate the other), a sine

wave oscillator and a noise generator. Audio processing includes a multi-mode filter, ring modulator, chorus and stereo delay. There are separate ADSR envelopes for the filter cutoff, output amplifier and waveset modulation. Wave selection within the waveset can also be modulated by LFO, velocity and key tracking. Finally, there is global vibrato and tuning.

The only parts of NanoWave that may be a bit unfamiliar are the wave players. These are sample players in what Reaktor refers to as Oscil mode. Each sample is treated like a series of waveforms of fixed length—the loop length specified in the sample file. The position of the waveform within the sample is selected using the slider at the left center of the Wave module Control Panel. The meter to its left indicates the current wave position, which can be modulated around the slider setting with the Wave Env, LFO, velocity or MIDI key. The wave player plays the waveform as an oscillator would, looping it at the rate corresponding to the desired pitch.

Reaktor comes with a number of wavesets contained in the sample map file named "WSM1" which is loaded automatically with the NanoWave Ensemble. These are set up so that each waveset contains 128 waveforms. You could use any sample as a waveset provided a loop of the intended waveform length is defined in the sound file. Alternately, you could choose the waveform length manually. The Ensemble NanoWave+ in the WIZOO Ensembles folder adds controls for this to each Wave module. When the *Man* button is on, the *Lp* knob sets the number of waveforms in the sample. (When the *Man* button is off, the loop information in the sample file is used as with the original NanoWave.)

Sonix

Instrument   Martin Brinkman
Sounds   Martin Brinkman

◎ **14**   Sonix

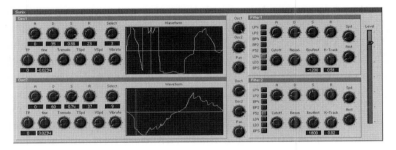

The Ensemble Control
Panel for Sonix—a
wavetable synthesizer
that allows you to
draw in your own
waveforms.

Sonix is the simplest of the factory library's wavetable synths. It uses Reaktor's new Audio Table Module to create and playback waveforms. Sonix contains two identical wavetable-oscillator sections followed by two multi-mode filters. The output of the oscillators is mixed at the input of each filter. The filters work in parallel and can be independently panned in the output mix.

Wavetable oscillators work by cycling through a list of numbers (the wavetable) at the rate necessary to create the desired pitch. Fortunately, right now you don't need to think about how this is done. We'll take a closer look in "WT-1: Wavetable Synthesis" on page 128. The short answer is that a normal ramp-up (i. e. sawtooth) is used to control the "read position" in the table.

So, where do wavetables come from? First of all, it's important to realize that Reaktor's Audio Table Module can hold many wavetables. In Sonix there are 128 wavetables for each oscillator and the active one is chosen with the *Select* knob (range 0 to 127). The quickest way to create or modify a wavetable is to simply draw in the Waveform window with the mouse. Try it while holding a note!

You can also use the Waveform window's context menu to load and save wavetables in several convenient forms including plain text (numbers separated by spaces), audio files (Wave or AIFF format) and Reaktor Table files (.ntf extension).

You can manipulate the data in the wavetable in various ways using the context menu (right-click on the PC, ctrl-click on the Mac) for the Waveform window. First use the Process sub-menu to enter Select mode; next use the mouse to select a section of the waveform; and finally use the Process sub-menu to transform the selection.

Each Sonix oscillator has its own amplitude ADSR envelope. It also has separate LFOs for vibrato (frequency) and tremolo (volume). The filters have their own ADSR envelope and LFO for controlling cutoff frequency. The filter mode buttons along the left actually switch between three filters: the standard Reaktor 4-pole filter (*LP4*, *LP2*, *BP4* and *BP2* modes), the Prophet 5 emulating Pro-52 filter (*P52* mode) and the Moog emulating Ladder filter (*LD4* and *LD3* modes). In case you haven't guessed it, *BPS* mode bypasses all filters.

WeedWacker

◎ **15**   WeedWacker

Instrument   Siegmar Kreie
Sounds   Siegmar Kreie, Vladislav Delay, Uwe G. Hoenig
Demo   Uwe G. Hoenig

The Ensemble Control Panel for Weed-Wacker—a physical modeling synth with complex modulation.

The heart of WeedWacker is a physical-modeling style oscillation circuit based on a two-ramp, pulse oscillator with feedback. Because an actual oscillator is used instead of the more common, feedback delay-line approach, the feedback is in the form of pulse-width modulation. First the oscillator's output is sent through a peak-EQ filter then through a mirror circuit which reshapes the wave by mirroring values outside of a given range to their inverses. Forget the details; the point is that you can get some seriously chaotic behavior.

▶ A word to the wise: ride your monitors when experimenting with WeedWacker—chaos breeds chaos.

The settings for the oscillator are contained in the top-center section of the control panel, in the section labeled "Osc". The *Up* and *Down* controls set the ramp times of the up and down portions of the pulse waveform. The *Min* and *Max* controls set the range of the mirror circuit. The *Shift* and *Res* controls set the frequency and resonance of the peak-EQ filter. The *Drive* control acts as a multiplier (i. e. overdrive) for the final output. The oscillator circuit also contains a noise generator used as a frequency modulator for the pulse oscillator. The *Noise* control sets the amount of noise FM and the effect is in fact similar to introducing noise into the output.

Notice that below each of the controls mentioned above is a small *Mod* knob. These knobs control the amount of modulation for the corresponding parameter from the modulation Matrix in the lower-left section of the Ensemble Control Panel. The modulation Matrix routes the output from the three LFOs to its right as well as the ADSR envelope generator above it. Each of the oscillator parameters can receive modulation from any one of these four sources. There is a second envelope generator, labeled "EG2", for controlling both the cutoff and highpass/lowpass mix of WeedWacker's multimode filter.

The WeedWacker Oscillator with oscilloscope.

▶ For better insight into the source of the WeedWacker mayhem, load the Ensemble WeedWackerOsc. This is the WeedWacker oscillator section without the Noise FM or any of the external modulation sources. The *Gate* button activates the oscillator at pitch A220. Use the Snapshots as a starting point then manipulate the various knobs.

The *Up* and *Down* knobs shape the ramps of the pulse wave to yield a waveform ranging from square to triangle. The *Boost* and *Reson* knobs set the height and width of the peak EQ's peak while the *Shift* knob sets the peak's frequency in semitones above and below A220. The *Max* and *Min* knobs set the mirror points. Finally, the *Feedback* slider controls the amount of pulse-width modulation feedback.

WeedWacker's Velo-Filter in the lower-right portion of the Ensemble Control Panel is a 2-pole resonant filter with highpass, bandpass and lowpass outputs. All three outputs as well as a mix of the highpass and lowpass signals are available as inputs to the stereo feedback-delay line that is WeedWacker's last processing stage. The diffusion controls, *Diff L* and *Diff R*, control the amount of feedback in the left and right delay lines respectively. The large Delay knobs set the delay times in note increments based on Reaktor's MIDI clock.

WeedWacker LFO rates can be synchronized to Reaktor's MIDI clock and its envelope generators can also be set to retrigger in sync with the clock. This feature is illustrated in a number of the WeedWacker snapshots.

Virtuator

Instrument   Uwe G. Hoenig, NI
Sounds   Uwe G. Hoenig, NI

⊚ **16**   Virtuator

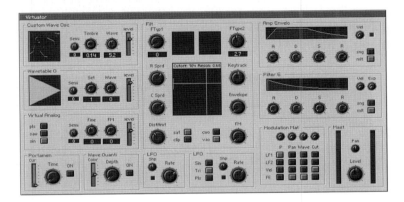

The Ensemble Control Panel for Virtuator—a wavetable synthesizer with xy filter control and a modulation matrix.

Virtuator takes advantage of some of Reaktor's newest Modules to offer several sophisticated variations on wavetable synthesis. It starts with three sound sources: a multi-mode, Virtual Analog oscillator, a Wavetable oscillator and a Custom Waveform oscillator that allows you to draw in your own waveforms.

Virtuator's Virtual Analog oscillator switches between square, sawtooth and parabolic waveforms. (A parabolic oscillator is a cheap imitation of a sine wave oscillator—it takes less CPU to calculate and sounds nearly the same). Each of these oscillators can be frequency modulated by the output of the Custom Waveform oscillator.

The Custom Waveform oscillator uses Reaktor's Audio Wavetable Module that we first saw in Sonix on page 53. In Virtuator, the table holds 12 waveforms and the *Wave* knob interpolates among them. The *Timbre* knob determines how much of the custom waveform is used (always looping from the left edge).

The Wavetable Oscillator uses a sample player in Oscil mode—a technique we first encountered in Nanowave on page 51. Typically the samples used in Oscil mode contain an evolving sequence of waveforms and the start points and lengths are chosen to be one waveform long. The sample player holds a map of up to 127 waveforms—the map in Virtuator contains 44.

Virtuator's Custom Wave and Wavetable oscillators with an Oscilloscope. Use the *Grab* button to grab the current Wavetable Osc wave into the selected position in the Custom Wave Osc.

▶ For a closer look at the Virtuator's Wavetable and Custom Wave oscillators, load the Ensemble VirtuatorOsc. The *Oscillator* switch toggles between the two oscillators for both audio and the oscilloscope. You can draw your own waveforms in the Custom Wave Osc or "grab" the current Wavetable Osc waveform by clicking the *Grab* button. Notice that you can also grab waves at "in between" positions and this will modify the waveforms at both ends of the interpolation. Also notice that you can grab only part of a wave by setting the *Timber* knob to a value less than 1 before grabbing. A grab feature has also been implemented in the Ensemble, Virtuator+, in the Factory folder inside the Ensembles folder on the wizoo cd. In that case, the wave is grabbed after the filter section.

The Custom Wave Osc wave selector scheme has been slightly modified here. The *Wave* knob selects the wave number in the table and the *fine* knob then interpolates between the selected wave and the next higher one.

Virtuator mixes the outputs of its three oscillators (using the *Level* sliders for each) and passes that through a quantizer and dual multi-mode filter circuits. The quantizer (which can be switched out) colors the waveform in two ways: it quantizes it (*Depth* control) and passes it through high-shelf EQ

(*Color* control). Both processes add harmonics to the signal and the best way to audition the effect is to use it on a simple sine wave.

Virtuator's Filter section (upper-center of the control panel) features two multi-mode filters with a variety of low-pass, bandpass and highpass outputs. The *FTyp1* knob selects among the first filter's outputs, smoothly scanning from no filtering at the left through the various filter types to 4-pole lowpass at the right. The output of the first filter is passed through distortion circuits (saturation or clipping) and a mix of the raw and distorted outputs is fed to the second filter. The *FTyp2* knob works just like the *FTyp1* knob relative to the output of the second filter.

One of the novel things about the Virtuator Filter is the use of Reaktor's new XY-Controller to set the two filters' cutoff frequency and resonance. Moving the crosshairs vertically affects resonance, moving them horizontally affects cutoff frequency. Both filters are affected and the *R Sprd* and *C Sprd* knobs set the relation (i. e. offset) between the two filters. Finally the filter cutoffs can be modulated by the ADSR Filter Envelope as well as the output from either the Custom Wave oscillator or the Virtual Analog oscillator.

Last but not least Virtuator has a couple of variable-shape LFOs and a Modulation Matrix for routing either LFO, MIDI Velocity and the Filter Envelope to pitch, pan, the waveform of the Wavetable Oscillator and the filter cutoff.

Sampling

Reaktor sampling runs the gamut from bread-and-butter multi-sample playing to advanced granular techniques. We'll have a look at several factory samplers here and examine each technique in detail in Chapter 4 "Building a Sampler" on page 141.

rAmpler

17   rAmpler

Instrument   NI
Sounds   Fritz Hildebrandt
Demo   Fritz Hildebrandt

rAmpler is very powerful sample manipulator containing two of Reaktor's sampler Modules: Sampler Loop and Sample Resynth. Sampler Loop gives you real-time control over sample looping, with controls for playback start-point (where playback starts when the sample is gated), loop start-point and loop length. Resynth is a grain player offering the same looping controls as Sampler Loop as well as pitch-shifting for individual grains. That gives you independent control of pitch and time.

The two samplers and their controls are at the upper-left of the Control Panel, separated by a switch to choose between them. Their controls are nearly identical except at the right end of the panel, where Resynth has its grain controls and Sampler Loop has controls for frequency modulation by an auxiliary oscillator or the re-synthesizer. The auxiliary oscillator, whose controls are at the bottom-center of the panel, is parabolic and has its own ADSR amplitude envelope. It can be mixed into the signal path or used to modulate the Sampler Loop.

The active sampler is processed by a 4-pole multi-mode filter (controls above the ax oscillator) then sent to the output. Its six filter modes can be mixed in any proportions and it has a built-in ADSR envelope for filter cutoff. There are two output processors: a stereo imager and our old friend, the StereoTDelay. The stereo imager acts on the sum of the sample player's right and left outputs, adding different very short delays to each output. The Master section's *Mo* button (bottom-left) toggles between stereo and left-channel-only for the sampler output. The stereo imager is useful in mono mode. Both effects can be switched off to save CPU.

rAmpler has two multi-waveform LFOs and a five-breakpoint envelope. Routers at the top-center of the Control Panel allow you to route each to pitch, cutoff, resonance, grain speed and grain size. The LFOs can be reset by incoming note-gates or the Master Clock in any note division.

After playing the demo MIDI file, select the Init Snapshot and explore rAmpler's sounds from your MIDI or computer keyboard. In the Master section, turn the *Aux* knob down and turn the *Sampler* knob up to get a feeling for how the two sample players differ. The Init Snapshot has everything else disabled except the filter. You can neutralize that by setting the *Cutoff* and *EnvA* knobs to zero and setting all the filter-mix knobs (along the top) to –60 except the *HP2* knob, which should be set to zero.

Triptonizer

Instrument Uwe G. Hoenig
Sounds D. Zelonky/Crank

Triptonizer uses another of Reaktor's resynthesis Modules—
the Sample Pitch Former. It analyzes the formants (i. e. resonant bands) of small fragments of the sample, then resynthe-
sizing the sound at any pitch, based on that analysis. In other
words, it constructs a new waveform based on its analysis of
the sample fragment and oscillates that waveform.

One interesting feature of the Sample Pitch Former is that
it allows you to pitch-shift the formants before resynthesis.
Another feature is that you can control the "scan rate"
through the sample being played independently of the resynthesis process. In that way, the Sample Pitch Former's processing is similar to granular techniques (as used in the Sample Resynth and Grain Cloud Modules), although Sample
Pitch Former's processing is not actually granular. The tip-off
is that there is no equivalent to the grain-size controls found
on the granular Modules.

Triptonizer gives you manual, envelope and LFO control
over the position in the sample being resynthesized and over
the amount of formant shifting. It also provides manual, key-

board and LFO control over the pitch of the resynthesized wave.

▶ Strictly speaking, the pitch of the resynthesized waveform is completely independent of the formant shift which affects the timbre (i. e. the wave shape). But, you'll find in many instances, especially if the original sample is pitched, that formant shifting has a significant effect on pitch.

If you turn the LFOs, envelopes and output processors (Drive, ModDelay and Reverb sections) off and play with the *wave* and *formant* sliders, you'll quickly get a feel for the effect of formant shifting versus pitch. (Make sure the *Noise* knob is full left—that provides random modulation of wave position.) After that, experiment with the LFOs and envelopes and you'll discover a wide variety of possibilities.

GrainStates

Instrument   Martin Brinkman
Sounds   Martin Brinkman

◎ **19**   GrainStates

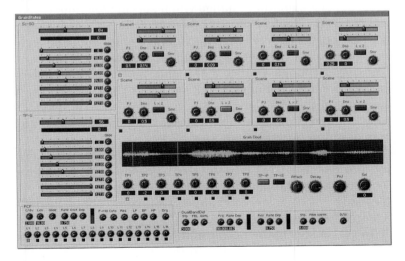

GrainStates is a granular sample player with built-in se-quencer. It uses Reaktor's very powerful Grain Cloud Module that provides granular playback of Reaktor sample maps (a. k. a. multi-samples). With Grain Cloud you get indepen-dent control of grain size and position, grain playback pitch and pitch slide, grain envelope attack and decay, time be-tween grains and output pan and amplitude. For a detailed look at Grain Cloud basics see "GS-2: Grain Cloud" on page 161.

Once you've got a feel for what Grain Cloud can do to a sample, the workings of the GrainStates Ensemble become fairly transparent. At the left of the Ensemble Control Panel are two eight-stage sequencers—the top one selects "Scenes", which you can think of as Grain Cloud presets and the bottom one transposes Grain Cloud's pitch or pitch-shift or both. (Grain Cloud's pitch and pitch-shift parameters are not part of the Scene.)

Both sequencers step in $\frac{1}{16}$-notes, synchronized to Reak-tor's clock, but instead of changing Scenes and transposi-tions at each step, they change when specific $\frac{1}{16}$-note counts are reached. The *Len* slider at the top of each sequencer sets the sequence length (i. e. the maximum count) while the eight *Pos* sliders below it set the counts at which the Scenes and transposes change. (Notice that higher positions don't neces-sarily have to have higher count settings.) The *Glide* knobs to the right of the *Pos* sliders are a very clever use of Reaktor's new Scanner Module to morph between adjacent Scene and transposition settings.

For good measure, GrainStates' author has thrown in one more sequencer. This is a standard $\frac{1}{16}$-note step sequencer for controlling the cutoff frequencies of two multi-mode fil-ters—one for each stereo channel. GrainStates' final stage is a stereo feedback delay.

To get an idea of the power of this accessible yet extremely elegant Ensemble, first listen to the three Snapshots in the Grain CloudTest Ensemble. These play the three samples used in GrainStates without any processing—i.e. the raw goods. Next listen to the GrainStates Snapshots and be amazed by what GrainStates does to those basic samples. Now it's your turn ...

Sequencing

Many Reaktor Ensembles have built-in sequencers that are driven by Reaktor's Master Clock. You must start the Master Clock using the Transport in the Ensemble Toolbar in order for the sequencers in these Ensembles to play. (See "Reaktor's Toolbars" on page 16.)

There are two ways to approach sequencing in Reaktor: using one of Reaktor's step-sequencer Modules and using event-tables. We'll look at each method in detail in Chapter 5 "Building a Sequencer" on page 165. Here we'll look at some ready-built sequencers using each method.

Cyclane

Instrument   Siegmar Kreie
Sounds   Rob Acid, NI
Demo   NI

⊚ **20** Cyclane

Cyclane illustrates the traditional approach to step-sequencing, whereas Obvious101 (see "Obvious101" on page 68) illustrates the more flexible, Event Table approach. Cyclane contains two 16-step sequencers. The one at the top-left is driving a sine wave based drum-synth whose controls are reminiscent of NewsCool (see "NewsCool" on page 71), but without NewsCool's randomization features. The one at the bottom drives a built-in FM synth with two parabolic carriers and a single triangle-wave operator.

Cyclane's output section (top-right) includes a multi-mode filter, dual resonators and a delay line. The little mixer has separate levels and effect sends for the top percussion row, the lower three percussion rows, the FM synth, an external input and all the effects outputs. The effects section is an excellent candidate for copying to your own Ensembles.

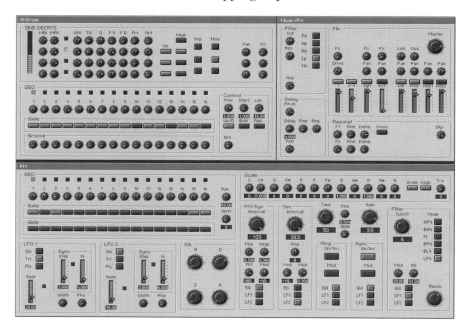

Cyclane's two step-sequencers are similar, but not identical. They do share the same clock controls, so let's look at that first. The clocking is controlled by the Control section to the right of the top sequencer. The sequencers run on Reaktor's Master Clock (so start the transport to hear anything). The Control section allows you

◆ to divide or multiply Reaktor's tempo by powers of two (i. e. 1, 2, 4, 8, …);

◆ to determine the starting position and length of the step-sequence;

◆ to set the direction (up, down, up-down) of the step-sequence;

◆ to apply a "groove" to the sequence. Groove is a very flexible delay control for selected sequence steps. Each step can have its own groove amount—controlled by the knobs in the Groove section and subject to the overall setting of the *Groov* knob in the Control section.

The drum sequencer has velocity (knobs) and gate (buttons) controls for each of the sixteen steps—just what you'd expect from a drum sequencer. The FM synth's sequencer has some unique features, though:

◆ The *Range* control to the right of the numbered pitch-knobs limits the pitch range of all knobs. Setting it to 12, for example, will limit each pitch knob to an octave. (The circuitry to accomplish that is not trivial—have a look.)

◆ The *Shift* knob offsets the FM sequence from the drum sequence.

◆ The Glide buttons apply glide (a. k. a. portamento) to the individual sequence steps. The amount of glide is controlled by the *Glide* knob in the tuning section of the FM synth.

◆ The Scale section—the sequencer's most unique—allows you to apply individual offsets (in semitones) to each of the twelve tones in the scale. That allows you to restrict the sequence to any scale you choose. And, the *Trans* knob allows you to shift the scale to any key.

Don't overlook the controls in Cyclane's FM synth. There's a lot to play around with there including ring modulation, oscillator hard-sync, a resonant multi-mode filter, a couple of LFOS and an ADSR envelope generator.

Obvious101

Instrument   Martin Brinkman
Sounds   Martin Brinkman

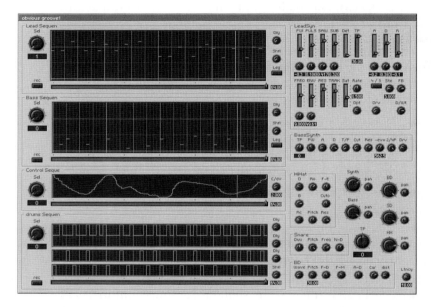

Obvious101 is another all-in-one sequencer with separate step-sequencers for built-in lead synth, bass synth and three-pad drum box. There's also a control sequencer that can be applied to various lead-synth parameters. In case you're counting, that's six sequencers in all and each can have up to 64 steps.

Each of Obvious101's sequencers is based on Reaktor's new Event Table Module. (For a detailed look at Event Tables and how they work see "Sqx-2: Event Table Sequencer" on page 171.) Each Event Table can hold 128 64-step sequences. The *Sel* knobs select which of the 128 sequences is active. The sequences can be edited on-screen with the mouse and if you right-click inside the sequence display, you can use the Process sub-menu to change to Select mode. In

Select mode, you select regions in the display (instead of editing values). Once a region is selected, use the Process submenu again to perform various modifications such as mirroring, rotating and scaling sequence values.

The horizontal sliders in each of the sequencer sections allow you to set the step-sequence lengths independently. The two pitch sequencers—lead and bass synth—have monitor buttons (*mon*), which when on, pass incoming MIDI notes directly to the synths. The *rec* buttons activate MIDI recording, whereby incoming MIDI note pitches are used to set the current sequencer step. There's no way to select a specific step, so you need to start the sequencer and record on the fly.

All the sequencers have shuffle (*shfl*) and delay (*dly*) controls. Shuffle (a. k. a. swing) delays every other note. Delay for the lead synth is a feedback-delay line for notes. The mix between the original and delayed sequence is controlled by the lead synth's *D/Wt* knob. The three controls above that control delay step-size ($\frac{1}{16}$ or $\frac{3}{64}$), delay-time in steps and feedback. In the other sequencers, the delay acts like a time-shift for the whole sequence.

The Control Sequencer works slightly differently than the rest. Its clock rate can be slowed from one-half to $\frac{1}{16}$ of the Master Clock rate using the *C/dv* knob. Its values can be applied in varying amounts to the lead synth's filter cutoff, envelope amount, resonance amount, keyboard tracking amount and delay parameters. The scaling is done using the knobs above the various parameters.

6-Pack

◎ **22**   6-Pack

Instrument   NI/monolake
Sounds   Rob Acid/NI
Demo   Rob Acid/NI

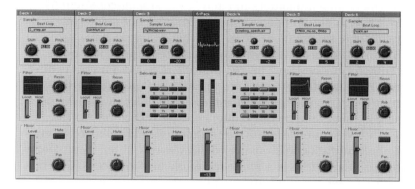

6-Pack is an array of six sample players, called "Decks", for creating complex loop and percussion effects. The four Beat Loop Decks (1, 2, 5 and 6) are intended to play sample loops and the two Sample Loop Decks (3 and 4) are for sequencing percussion samples. Pick any Snapshot, mute all the Decks then un-mute them one at a time and you'll quickly get the idea.

The Beat Loop Decks use Reaktor's Beat Loop Module to automatically slice the loops up and resynthesize them during playback. That gives you independent control of loop playback speed and pitch.

The Beat Loop Module holds up to 128 samples at a time and the small selector knob below the sample name display selects which of the map samples are played. (Double-click the name display to add and replace samples.) The *Shift* knob controls the sample start point in ¹⁄₁₆-note steps and the *Pitch* knob transposes the sample without affecting the loop time.

The Beat Loop Decks contain an unusual filter section, which plays a large part in characterizing their sound. The signal is passed through right and left pairs of resonant high-pass and lowpass filters in series. Each pair of filters forms a bandpass filter with a variable width band (the width is the difference between the frequencies of the high and lowpass filters). Finally, there is a randomizer for slowly randomizing all filters' cutoff frequencies. The amount of randomization is controlled by the *Rob* knob.

The Sample Loop Decks use a ¹⁄₁₆-note step sequencer to trigger sample playback from Reaktor's Sample Loop Module, which is a basic sample player. The same controls—sample select, start point and pitch—are provided, but this time there is no filter section and no resynthesis. Changing the pitch does change the sample length. The sequencer contains 16 buttons for activating sequence steps.

NewsCool

Instrument   NI
Sounds   NI

⊚ **23**   NewsCool

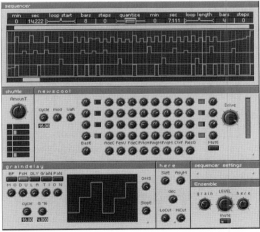

NewsCool Ensemble Control Panel. Gate sequencer at top, shuffle and drum synth in the middle, grain delay, reverb and output mix on the bottom.

NewsCool is a four-voice drum synthesizer with built-in gate-sequencer. For good measure, there is a real-time random-

izer for the drum synth parameters (see "Control Randomizer" on page 200 for a detailed look at control randomization), a grain delay effect and a reverb unit (named "h e r e").
Let's start with a look at the drum synth.

   Each voice of the drum synth is based on a triangle wave
oscillator and a 2-pole, resonant bandpass filter. There are
also decay envelopes for the oscillator's amplitude and pitch.
Each voice can be either a source or a destination for both
ring and frequency modulation of the oscillator. Whether a
voice is a source or destination is controlled by the knobs labeled Ring Mod and Freq Mod in the illustration. When the
knob is in the left half of its range it controls incoming modulation amount. When in the right half of its range it controls
modulation output (pre-mix). (For no modulation input or
output, set the knob to its mid position.) The sum of the modulation sources is applied to each of the modulation destinations.

Controls for one voice
of NewsCool's drum
sequencer.

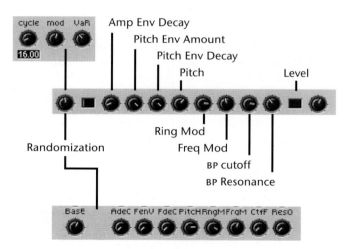

Each of the synthesizer's controls can be automated in sync
with the sequencer clock. The fifth row of knobs (below the
synth controls) is for setting the amount of automation for

the knobs above it. The *Randomization* knob at the left of each row of synth controls sets the amount of randomization for that row. The *Base* knob sets the center point around which randomization occurs. The controls shown in the upper left of the illustration are global controls for the randomizer. The *cycle* knob sets the step timing in $1/96$-notes. The *mod* knob is a global amount control and the *VaR* knob sets the amount of random variation.

▶ The best way to get a feel for the synth controls is to loop a part of the sequence where at least two rows are active. Turn down the levels of all but one of the active rows and start the sequencer playing (using the Toolbar's Master Clock buttons). First tweak the envelope, pitch and filter controls of the audible row. Then set its frequency or ring modulation controls to receive and set the other active row's modulation controls to send. Next, tweak the send row's controls to see the effect of modulation. Finally, play with the various randomization controls, watch the knobs dance and listen for the effect.

NewsCool's sequencer uses four Event Table Modules to generate four velocity-gate sequences. Each bar in the table gates the corresponding synth module with velocity proportionate to the height of the bar. The gray scroll bar at the top sets the loop's position and length relative to the Event Table graphics. The gray scroll bar at the bottom sets the Event Table graphic's zoom and position (i. e. what's visible). Click on the right edge of either scroll bar to change its length. Click anywhere else to change its position.

▶ The *Shuffle* controls to the left of the synthesizer section allow you to create a shuffle pattern of up to six steps. The small squares to the left indicate the current shuffle step. The rectangles on the right are for both setting the shuffle amount (left/right motion) and turning the step on and off (up/down motion). The amount is always relative to the *AmounT* knob.

The GrainDelay section is made up of a 2-pole bandpass filter followed by a granular delay line. The granular delay breaks the signal into grains, which can be delayed, pitch shifted and panned across the stereo field. There is a little step sequencer for modulating each of these parameters as well as the grain size and bandpass filter frequency. The scope displays the modulation pattern for the parameter selected by the radio buttons above the modulation amount knobs. (For details on how to create radio buttons in Reaktor, see "Radio Buttons" on page 197.)

▶ In case that description leaves you cold, turn the *grain* knob fully up in the Ensemble sub-panel (for a 100% wet mix) and play with the GrainDelay controls. This is one of the most creative features of the NewsCool Ensemble.

NewsCool's reverb section (named "h e r e") is straightforward. Extreme low settings for the *SizE* knob along with moderate *dec* knob settings provide a sort of resonator effect. In conjunction with some grain delay (which precedes the reverb in the signal path) the effect can be quite unique.

There's one more set of NewsCool controls to deal with—the Sequencer Settings. These are only visible in the Instrument Control Panel, which you can open by double-clicking the empty sub-panel in the Ensemble Control Panel window. At the left is a miniature representation of the four gate sequences. The controls in the middle let you set the maximum number of steps (from 32 to 2048), the note-value of a single step (from whole-notes to 1/96-notes) and the number of steps in a bar. The controls on the right display the maximum sequence length and adjust the behavior of the zoom scroll bar.

NewsCool's sequencer settings Instrument Control Panel.

Effects Processing
GeekFX

◎ **24** GeekFX

Instrument   NI (jr)
Sounds   NI (jr)
Demo   NI (jr)

Think of GeekFX as three multi-effects boxes providing distortion, filter and delay effects. Each effects section contains
multiple effects, but only one can be used at a time. Each of
the effects sections can be turned on or off independently
and turning sections off will save significant CPU.

At the top of GeekFX there is a section containing a sample
player, a gate module for pre-processing, a mixer for the
source and the three effects and an output equalizer. Again,
each of these can be turned off if not needed. To audition the
effects, select a sample and start the sample player playing.

Each of the effects sections is divided into three sections.
The left section is identical for each and includes an input
mixer, a low cut filter, an LFO, an envelope follower and a
modulation mixer. The modulation mix is applied to the vari-

ous effects in different ways. At the center of each effect section is a vertical switch for selecting the active effect. The actual effects are arranged on the right.

The Distortion section contains six effects: overdrive, two forms of bit reduction, ring modulation, a pitch-shifter emulation named ssb (for single sideband) and a defective cable emulation. ssb is the unique effect in this batch.

There are five effects in the Filter section: a four pole (24dB/octave) multi-mode filter with its own lfo, a resonant bandpass filter, an eight band eq, a vowel morphing filter (a parallel array of notch filters) and a feedback-delay resonator. Vowel Morph and Resonator are the hands-down winners here.

The Delay section also contains five effects: a phaser, a flanger, two and three tap delays and a granular resynthesis module called Pitch Delay—try it!

▶ Each of GeekFX effects sections is a self-contained Reaktor Instrument and therefore can be used in your own Ensembles. For convenience, these Instruments have been saved in the Instruments folder on the WIZOO CD as GFX Distortion.ism, GFX Filter.ism and GFX Delay.ism.

3 Building a Synthesizer

Now that we've had a good look at what others have done with Reaktor, it's time to do it ourselves. First, we'll build a basic subtractive synthesizer in the simplest way. We'll use that as a starting point for adding refinements and enhancements. Finally we'll move into other synthesis techniques.

The following chapters will take a similar approach to building samplers, sequencers and effects processors. In all cases, our aim is not to build the most sophisticated, feature-laden Ensemble possible—we'll leave that to you. What we will endeavor to do is lead you step-by-step to the edge of the cliff.

Structure Overview

In "Ensemble? Control Panel? Structure?" on page 11 we took a brief look at Reaktor's structural organization. The highest level is the Ensemble and there is one and only one Ensemble open in Reaktor at a time. Ensembles are made up of Instruments, Macros and Modules connected by wires.

Modules are Reaktor's basic building blocks. They are part of the Reaktor application (they are not files on your hard drive) and are created using Reaktor's Insert menu or the context menu that opens when you right-click (ctrl-click on the Mac) in the empty space in any Structure window (see illustration).

The Modules context menu for creating new Modules in any Structure. To create a new Module, right-click in the empty space in a Structure window, then select the desired module from one of the sub-menus.

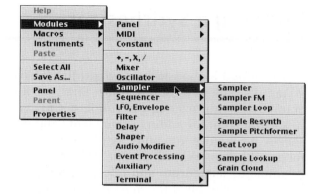

Instruments and Macros are organizational Structures containing Modules, other Instruments and Macros and the wires connecting them. How you organize Instruments and Macros (and whether you use them at all, for that matter) is completely up to you. We'll illustrate the most common techniques here. As you'll see from these and the factory Ensembles, there are many approaches, but one thing is for sure:

▶ If you try to do everything on the Module level without ever dealing with Instruments and Macros, you'll quickly wind up with an unwieldy tangle of objects and wires with no hope of understanding or modifying what you've done at a later date.

Every Reaktor Ensemble must have two Modules: Audio In and Audio Out. You can not delete these and you can not have more than one of each. It is also advisable to keep the optional Master and Tune controls that are present in the factory New Ensemble (see illustration).

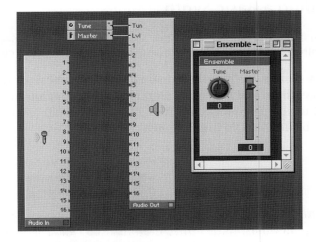

Reaktor's New Ensemble contains the required Audio In and Audio Out Module as well as optional *Master* and *Tune* controls. Its Control Panel is shown in the inset on the right.

Most Instruments, Macros and Modules have terminals (inputs and outputs) for wiring them together. These come in two varieties: audio (black) and event (red). The technical difference is the rate at which Reaktor "scans" them during processing. Audio terminals are processed at the audio sampling rate (which is displayed in the Ensemble Tool Bar—see "Reaktor's Toolbars" on page 16) and event terminals are processed at the control rate, which is set in the Settings menu. The control rate is much lower than the audio sampling rate and therefore, event inputs require much less CPU processing.

▶ You can wire an event output into an audio input, but not vice versa. When you need to do that, you can use the A to E Module (in the Auxiliary section) to convert the audio signal to an event signal.

Building a Basic Synth

▶ You'll find the synthesizers in this section—BS-1 through BS-6—in the Synthesizers folder inside the Ensembles folder on the WIZOO CD.

In this section we'll build a one-oscillator synthesizer with a lowpass filter and two ADSR (Attack, Decay, Sustain and Release) envelope generators. Along the way you'll learn most of the basic tricks to building Reaktor Ensembles.

Ensemble Control Panel window for the basic synth, BS-3, featuring a single oscillator, lowpass filter and two ADSR envelopes.

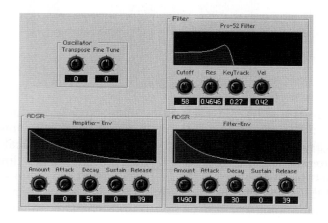

BS-1: Oscillator and ADSR

The Ensemble Structure for BS-1 is shown in the illustration. Notice that it is just like Reaktor's New Ensemble except that there is one more object, the Instrument named "Basic Synth".

The first job in building this Ensemble is to open the New Ensemble and add an empty Instrument to it. You add a new Instrument to an Ensemble in its Structure window using either Reaktor's Insert menu or using the context menu that pops up when you right-click in any empty space in the Structure window. When you select Instrument from the menu, an open dialog appears allowing you to search your hard drive for the desired object. You'll find Instruments named "New" in both the Reaktor factory library and in the Instruments folder on the WIZOO CD.

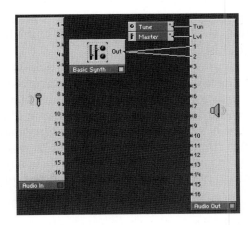

BS-1 Ensemble Structure. The Instrument named "Basic Synth" has been added to the Reaktor New Ensemble.

▶ The process is the same for adding any new structural element (Instrument, Macro or Module) in any Structure window. Instruments and Macros are stored on your hard drive. Modules are part of the Reaktor program and are created using sub-menus of the context menu.

The next step is to select the Instrument just created and open its Structure window. You can do this from the Instrument Toolbar or from the context menu that opens when you right-click on the Instrument.

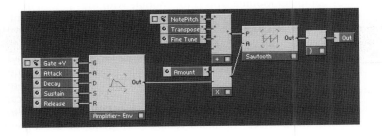

The Structure window of the Basic Synth Instrument in the BS-1 Ensemble.

The illustration above shows the Structure of the completed Basic Synth Instrument in the BS-1 Ensemble. Of course, the new Instrument Structure window you just opened is empty. All the objects shown here are Modules, making this a very simple Structure with no embedded Macros or Instruments. (As mentioned above, you can't get away with this in more sophisticated Ensembles.)

Here are step-by-step instructions for building the Basic Synth Instrument. In future sections, we will give much more abbreviated instructions which will draw on the details given here. If you've never built anything in Reaktor, I suggest you follow the step-by-step instructions. If you have some Reaktor experience, then just scan this section to see if there is anything new to you. The finished Ensemble is named "BS-1" in the Synthesizers folder inside the Ensembles folder on the WIZOO CD.

▶ Caveat Emptor: Save the Ensemble to your hard drive at regular intervals during the construction process.

The first thing to do is create an output for the Instrument so that it can be wired into the Ensemble's Audio Output Module:

1 Use the Terminal sub-menu of the Modules menu to create an Audio Out terminal. This is the Module you see at the far right of the Structure and is how the Instrument's output is connected to the Ensemble's Audio Out Module in the Ensemble Structure.

2 Use the Auxiliary sub-menu of the Modules menu to create an Audio Voice Combiner Module. This is the Module with the "}" icon in the illustration. Draw a wire from the Audio Voice Combiner's output into the Out terminal's input.

▶ An Audio Voice Combiner Module is necessary before any audio output for any polyphonic Instrument. This tells Reaktor, which carries out separate calculations for each of an Instrument's voices, to combine these calculations into a single output signal. Note that you can set up an Instrument's number of voices in its Properties or on the Instrument Toolbar (see "Reaktor's Toolbars" on page 16). It's a good idea to also use an Audio Voice Combiner with monophonic Instruments because you may want to make the Instrument polyphonic at a later date.)

The next step is to create an oscillator for the synth:

3 Use the Oscillator sub-menu of the Modules menu to create a Sawtooth Module. This is one of Reaktor's simplest oscillators, with a single output for the sawtooth wave and two inputs: one for the oscillator's pitch and the other for the oscillator's amplitude. Draw a wire from the Sawtooth Module's output into the Audio Voice Combiner Module's input.

These steps are for controlling the oscillator's pitch via MIDI along with semi-tone transpose and fine tuning controls:

4 Use the +,−,X,/ sub-menu of the Modules menu to create an Event Add 4 Module. This Module will add four Event signals (see "Structure Overview" on page 77 for a description of Audio and Event signals). We will use three of its inputs to provide MIDI keyboard control as well as coarse and fine tuning for the oscillator. The fourth input will be used later to add LFO-vibrato (see "BS-5: LFO and Sample-and-Hold" on page 94). Draw a wire from the Event Add 4 Module's output into the Sawtooth Module's *P* input.

▶ Many Modules have pitch inputs labeled *P*. These exponentially convert MIDI Note numbers to frequency with MIDI Note number 69 corresponding to A440 (i. e. 440Hz). Many Modules also have frequency inputs labeled *F* which interpret their inputs linearly as frequency in Hertz.

5 Use the MIDI sub-menu of the Modules menu to create a Note Pitch Module. This Module's output carries all incoming MIDI Note numbers. Draw a wire from the Note Pitch Module's output into the top input of the Event Add 4 Module.

6 Place the cursor over the second input of the Event Add 4 Module and right-click. Select Create Control from the context menu that appears (see illustration). This will create a Control Panel control named *Add 2* already wired into the second input of the Event Add 4 Module. Change the settings to those shown in the illustration. (Function tab: Label to "Transpose", Range Max to 36, Range Min to −36, Step to 1. Appearance tab: Size to Medium, Visible in Ensemble is checked.) The range of −36 to 36 allows a three octave transposition up or down and the step size of 1 results in semitone steps.

Use an input's context menu (left) to automatically create controls wired to the input. Use a control's context menu to set up its function (middle) and appearance (right).

▶ When you create controls automatically this way, Reaktor will take a guess at the proper name and range for the control. Often you will want to change these as well as the control's appearance. You do so using the control's context menu (right-click).

7 Repeat step 6 for the third input of the Event Add 4 Module to create a fine tuning control. The range for this knob should be –0.5 to 0.5 in steps of 0.01. This covers the full range between the semitone steps of the *Transpose* knob.

Applying an envelope to an oscillator's amplitude is one of several ways to control amplitude. Alternatives include multiplying the output signal by the envelope value, using the envelope to control an amplifier and using the envelope to control mixer levels.

The final steps add an ADSR envelope to control the oscillator's amplitude:

8 Use the +,–,X,/ sub-menu of the Modules menu to create an Audio Mult 2 Module. This Module will multiply two audio signals and we'll use it to multiply the output of the ADSR envelope generator by the value of an amount control. Wire the Audio Mult 2 Module's output to the oscillator's *A* input.

▶ All of the +,–,X,/ Modules come in both audio and event varieties. Recall that the only difference between audio and event signals is the sampling rate with which Reaktor processes them—event signals require much less processing. We've used an Audio Mult 2 Module here to match the ADSR Envelope's output and the oscillator's amplitude input (A). In the case of the ADSR Envelope Module, this results in smoother enveloping and in the case of the oscillator, it also allows for amplitude (AM) and ring (RM) modulation.

9 As in step 6, place the cursor over the first input of the Audio Mult 2 Module and right-click. Select Create Control from the context menu that appears. That will create a Control Panel control named *Mult 1* wired into the first input of the Audio Mult 2 Module. Open the control's Properties and in the Functions section, change the Label to *Amount*, the range minimum to 0 and the step size to 0.01. In the Appearance section change the knob's size to medium.

10 Select ADSR from the LFO/Envelope sub-menu of the Modules menu to create an ADSR Envelope Module. Open its Properties window and in the Appearance section check Visible in Instrument and Visible in Ensemble. This will cause a graphic of the ADSR shape to appear on the Instrument and Ensemble Control Panels. Also change its Pixel in X Size parameter to 200 and change its name to "Amplifier-Env". Wire the ADSR Envelope Module's output into the second input of the Audio Mult 2 Module.

11 As in steps 6, 7 and 9, create controls for the bottom four inputs (labeled *A, D, S* and *R*) of the ADSR Envelope Module. In this case, all the default control properties will be ok, but change each of the knob sizes to medium.

12 Select Gate from the MIDI sub-menu of the Modules menu to create a MIDI Gate Module. Wire the Gate Module's output into the *G* input of the ADSR Envelope Module. Double-click the Gate Module to open its Properties and change its name to "Gate +V" to indicate that Module's output will reflect the MIDI Note-On velocity. Note that its Range and MIDI parameters match the illustration.

▶ The Range and MIDI parameters of the Gate Module allow you to scale the Gate Module's velocity range. Setting the Range Min and Max both to one results in no velocity sensitivity. Creating velocity sensitivity this way only works if the receiving Module's gate (*G*) input automatically scales its output by the incoming gate value, as does the ADSR Envelope Module.

All that's left to do now is clean up the Control Panel, connect the audio output and give our basic synth a test drive.

13 Go to the Ensemble Structure window and wire the Instrument output (labeled *Out*) to both the *1* and *2* inputs of the Audio Output Module. (Even though our basic synth is mono, we want output in both channels.)

14 Select the Instrument and open its Properties window using the context menu or the Properties button in the Instrument Toolbar. Change the Instrument's name to "Basic Synth" and at the bottom of the Properties window check Controls Visible in Ensemble. (That ensures that each of the controls we've created will appear in the Ensemble

Control Panel even if we forgot to check "Visible in Ensemble" in the individual control's Properties.

Ensemble Control
Panel for BS-1.

15 Open the Ensemble Control Panel. (Make sure the menu at the left end of the Instrument Toolbar displays "Ensemble", then click the Control Panel icon in the Toolbar.) Unlock the Control Panel (to allow you to move the controls around) by clicking the Unlock button (pad-lock icon) in the Ensemble Toolbar until it is not indented. Now rearrange the individual controls to match the Basic Synth Control Panel in the illustration. Finally, move the Ensemble Control Panel with the *Master* and *Tune* controls next to the Basic Synth Control Panel as shown.

16 Double-click the Basic Synth Control Panel. The bad news is that you have to arrange the controls separately in the Ensemble and Instrument Control Panels. The good news is that you can have different visual arrangements in these panels (including different sets of visible controls).

17 Lock the Control Panels again in the Toolbar. (When the Control Panels are unlocked, using the mouse moves the controls around rather than changing their settings.)

◎ **25** BS-1

Congratulations! You have built a working synthesizer in Reaktor. Play your MIDI keyboard, tweak the knobs and enjoy your new powers as a master of the universe. (Oh and don't forget to save your work.)

BS-2: Filter

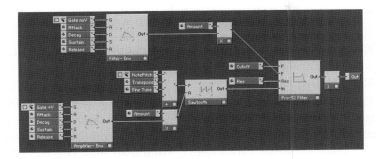

Instrument Structure window for the BS-2 Ensemble, which adds a resonant low-pass filter with its own ADSR envelope.

BS-1 lacks many things, but the most glaring is a filter—subtractive synthesis is all about filters, right? So that's our next job and now that you've waded through the step-by-step approach, we'll graduate to a more descriptive presentation.

The illustration shows the end result. The components of BS-1, which you just built, are in the lower-left portion of the Structure. The filter (named "Pro-52 Filter" because it is modeled after the filter in the Sequential Prophet 5 hardware synthesizer) has been wired between the oscillator and the Audio Combiner Module on the right.

1   Create the filter by selecting "Pro-52" from the Filter sub-menu of the Modules menu. (No surprises here.) Open its Properties window, make it visible in the Ensemble and Instrument and change its Pixel in X size to 164. (This makes a graphic of the filter visible.)

2   Create the *Cutoff* and *Res* controls using the context menu for the filter's *P* and *Res* inputs. The only changes necessary are the knob sizes (medium), control names (*Cutoff* instead of the default *P Cutoff*) and visibility in the Ensemble Control Panel.

3   Use the mouse to select all the elements of the amplitude envelope (i. e. the ADSR Envelope Module, all its controls, the Gate +V Module and the Audio Mult 2 and *Amount* control Modules.) Then select Copy and Paste, respectively, from Reaktor's Edit menu to create a similar envelope for the filter cutoff. Wire the output of the new Audio Mult 2 Module into the filter's *F* input. Double-click the Gate Module, change its range minimum to 1 and change its name to "Gate noV". (Typically, the filter cutoff does not respond to MIDI Note Velocity, but

if you prefer otherwise skip the last step.) Finally, rename the ADSR Envelope Module to "Filter -Env".

26 BS-2

4 Rearrange the new controls in both the Ensemble and Instrument Control Panel windows and you're done.

Take this one for a spin and don't forget to save your work.

BS-3: Using Macros

This is a good time to start encapsulating sections of the synth into Macros. That makes complex Ensembles easier to understand, easier to edit and easier to rip off (i. e. swap logical units between Ensembles). We'll also add key tracking for the filter cutoff and velocity sensitivity for the filter resonance.

The first thing we need in order to use Macros is an empty Macro. You do this in the same way you added an empty Instrument before creating BS-1. Right-click in an empty portion of the Instrument Structure window, select Macro from the context menu, then if the Macro named "Empty" appears as a choice on the sub-menu, choose it. Otherwise choose Open and find the Empty Macro in either the Reaktor library or in the Macros folder on the WIZOO CD.

Once you have the empty Macro, open its Structure and create an Audio Output terminal (see step 1 of "BS-1: Oscillator and ADSR" on page 82). Then return to the Instrument Structure window, select the Macro and use Copy and Paste to make three copies. You should now have four empty Macros with audio outputs. We'll use these for the two ADSR envelopes, the oscillator and the filter.

Drag with the mouse to select the modules in the amplitude ADSR envelope.

1 Select the modules that make up the amplitude ADSR envelope for the oscillator as indicated in the illustration. Cut these using the Edit menu or by typing ⌨ctrl⌨X (⌘⌨X on the Mac). Then double-click one of the empty Macros to open its Structure window and paste them into the Structure by using the Edit menu or the key command ⌨ctrl⌨P (⌘⌨P on the Mac). Wire the output of the Audio Mult 2 Module into the Audio Output Terminal Module. Finally, right-click an empty space in the Macro's Structure window and open its Properties from the context menu. Name it "ADSR" and in the Appearance section make it visible in the Ensemble.

2 Do the same for the Modules making up the ADSR envelope for the filter cutoff.

3 Do the same for the oscillator and its pitch control Modules as illustrated. Once these are pasted in a Macro create an Audio Input Module, name it "Am" and wire it into the Oscillator Module's A input. Finally create an Event Input Module, name it "Pm" and wire it into the fourth input of the Event Add 4 Module.

4 Do the same for the remaining Modules except the Audio Voice Combiner and Audio Output Terminal (i. e. for those associated with the filter). This time create two new Audio Input Modules. Name one "In" and wire it to the Filter Module's In input. Name the other "Fm" and wire it to the Filter Module's F input.

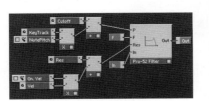

Filter enhancements for cutoff frequency key tracking and resonance velocity sensitivity.

5 The next step is to add key tracking for the filter cutoff frequency and velocity sensitivity for the filter resonance. The required Modules and their wiring are shown in the illustration. For key tracking, this amounts to multiplying the MIDI Note number (Note Pitch Module) by the desired tracking amount (KeyTrack Fader Module) and adding the result to the cutoff frequency (Cutoff Fader Module). For velocity sensitivity it amounts to multiplying the MIDI Note-on Velocity (On. Vel Module) by the desired tracking amount (Vel Fader Module) and adding the result to the resonance (Res Fader Module). The Fader Modules are found on the Panel sub-menu of the Modules menu. The Note Pitch and On. Vel Module are found on the MIDI sub-menu. The X and + Modules are found on the +,−,X,/ sub-menu.

6 Finally, go to the Instrument Structure window and wire the four Macros together as shown in the illustration. Open the Ensemble Control Panel window and rearrange the Macros and controls as shown in the illustration.

▶ If not all controls and Macro borders are visible in the Ensemble Control Panel, open the Instrument Properties and turn Controls Visible in Ensemble off and back on. That will turn the Visible in Ensemble Property on for all controls and Macros in the Instrument.

7 Open the Instrument Control Panel window and rearrange the Macros and controls in that window, too. (Remember, you need to temporarily unlock the Control Panels in the Toolbar to move things around then lock them again to use the controls.)

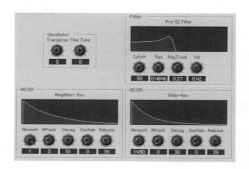

⊚ **27** BS-3

We now completed our basic synth. Before we beef it up a bit, play around with it, perhaps creating some snapshots and don't forget to save it to your hard drive.

Basic Synth Enhancements

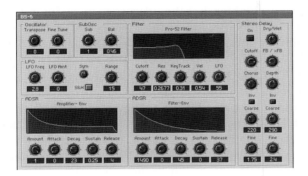

Control Panel for the final basic synthesizer, BS-6. Enhancements include a sub-oscillator, LFO/Sample-and-Hold and a pilfered stereo, cross-feedback delay.

In this section, we'll add three features to our basic synth: a sub-oscillator, an LFO with Sample-and-Hold and a stereo, cross-feedback delay extracted from the ManyMood Ensemble (see "ManyMood" on page 34).

BS-4: Sub-Oscillator

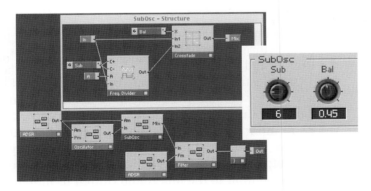

Structure of the BS-4 Instrument, the Structure of the sub-oscillator Macro and the sub-oscillator Control Panel.

In the early days of analog synthesis, oscillators were both expensive and difficult to keep in tune. Having several of them multiplied both the cost and the tuning problem and a common solution to both problems was to use frequency divider circuitry to produce sub-harmonics instead of a second (or sometimes third) oscillator. Of course, none of those problems exist in Reaktor, but the process is more interesting and instructive than simply plugging in a second oscillator.

The illustration shows both the BS-4 Instrument Structure window and the sub-oscillator (SubOsc) Macro Structure window. The SubOsc controls are also shown in the inset.

Aside from the inputs, outputs and controls, there are only two Modules needed: the Frequency Divider from the Audio Modifier sub-menu of the Modules menu and the Crossfade Module from the Mixer sub-menu. (Note that there is also a Frequency Divider in the Event Processing sub-menu, but because we're dealing with audio here, we need the audio version.)

▶ Instead of step-by-step instructions as in the previous sections, we'll now graduate to a summary format. If you find the going a little rough at first, remember you'll find each of these Ensembles in the Synthesizers folder inside the Ensembles folder on the WIZOO CD.

Here's how to build the sub-oscillator and insert it into the BS-3 Ensemble to build BS-4:

◆ Create an empty Macro (see "BS-3: Using Macros" on page 88). Create three terminals: two Audio Inputs and one Audio Output and name them "In", "A" and "Mix", respectively (see illustration). Next create the Crossfade and Frequency Divider Modules. Wire the *In* Audio Input terminal into both the Crossfade's *In1* input and the Frequency Divider's *In* input. Wire the *A* Audio Input terminal into the Frequency Divider's *A* input. Wire the Frequency Divider's output into the Crossfade's *In2* input. Wire the Crossfade's output to the Mix Audio Output terminal.

◆ Right-click the Crossfade's *X* input to create the balance control. (You'll need to rename it and change the knob size to medium.) Right-click on the Frequency Divider's *C+* input to create the sub-harmonic control. Change its range minimum to 1 (by default it is 1.0001) and wire it also into the Frequency Divider's *C−* input. Change its name to "Sub" and its size to medium.

The Frequency Divider Module requires a little explanation. It sends out a pulse wave whose value jumps between A and −A (where A is the amplitude setting). It counts zero-crossings of the audio signal at the *In* input. It holds the positive value for the number of zero-crossings set by the *C+* input and holds the negative value for the number of zero-crossings at the *C−* input. If the incoming waveform has two zero-crossings per cycle (one going up and one going down, as a sine wave does) the frequency of the Frequency Divider's pulse wave output will be twice the frequency of that waveform, divided by the sum of the values at the *C+* and *C−* inputs. (Note that the Frequency Divider always rounds these input values to integers.)

Since we've wired the *Sub* control to both inputs, the frequency of the Frequency Divider's pulse wave output will be the frequency of the main oscillator divided by the value of the *Sub* control. For example, when the *Sub* value is 2, it will be an octave lower than the main oscillator and when the value is 3, it will be an octave and a fifth lower, etc. Since the sub-oscillator is always lower in frequency, it will take on the role of the fundamental and you may need to transpose the main oscillator to match the keys you're playing to what you're hearing. For example, if the *Sub* value is 3, transpose the main oscillator up a fifth (7 semitones).

▶ Can you think of a way to make these transposes automatically linked to the Sub control? (Hint: consider using the Event Table Module.)

◆ Make sure the Macro and the new controls are visible in the Ensemble Control Panel and rearrange them as necessary in both the Instrument and Ensemble Control Panels.

◆ All that's left is to wire the SubOsc Macro into the Ensemble Structure. Wire the amplifier ADSR into the sub-oscillators *A* input. (Recall that this controls the amplitude of the Frequency Divider's pulse wave output.) Wire the oscillator's output into the sub-oscillators *In* input. (Recall that this goes both to the Frequency Divider and one of the Crossfade inputs.) Wire the sub-oscillator's *Mix* output into the filter's *In* input (replacing the wire from the oscillator).

⊚ **28** BS-4

You're done—play and save as usual.

BS-5: LFO and Sample-and-Hold

LFO and Sample-and-Hold Structure and Control Panel windows in BS-5.

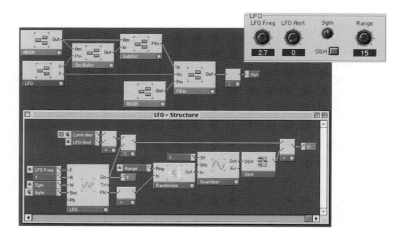

LFO (Low Frequency Oscillator) and sample-and-hold circuits were nearly universal features of early analog synths. Typically, the LFO used a sine wave oscillator running at sub-audio frequencies to modulate an audio oscillator's pitch (vibrato) or output amplifier level (tremolo). Later, filter cutoff frequency and oscillator pulse-width (PW) also became common targets.

Sample-and-hold circuits sampled the output of a noise generator at regular intervals and applied it to oscillator pitch to produce a random step-sequence. It was common to "quantize" the sample-and-hold output to semitone note values. The LFO was usually used to "clock" the sample-and-hold circuit (i. e. control the speed of the random step-sequence), which is why these two circuits are typically associated with each other.

Here is a summary of the LFO/sample-and-hold circuitry for our basic synth (see illustration):

◆ As always, start by creating an empty Macro. You'll need two Event Out terminals, labeled "O" and "F" for sending the LFO output to the oscillator and filter separately. (The reason for separate outputs is allow the filter cutoff to be LFO'd independently of the sample-and-hold output.)

◆ The main Modules are the LFO (LFO, Envelope sub-menu), the Randomizer and the Quantizer (Event Processing sub-menu). You'll also need an Event Switch 1 Module (Panel sub-menu) to turn the sample-and-hold on and off.

◆ The LFO offers three waveform outputs: sine, triangle and pulse. We'll use the pulse output for the sample-and-hold clock and the sine output for the LFO signal. Wire the LFO's *Sin* output to the *F* output terminal you just created. (We'll deal with the *O* output in a bit.) Use the context menu for the LFO's *F* input to create the LFO Frequency control. Use a Constant with value one for the LFO's amplitude (*A* input).

◆ The LFO Module provides a *Snc* input for resetting the LFO (i. e. starting at the beginning of the waveform). Having each MIDI Note reset the LFO is a common option, which we'll employ here for the benefit of the sample-and-hold. Create a MIDI Gate Module (MIDI sub-menu) and wire it to the LFO's *Snc* input.

◆ The LFO Module's *W* input controls the symmetry of the sine and triangle waveforms as well as the width of the pulse waveform. Use the context menu for the LFO's *W* input to create the LFO symmetry control. The default value range is −1 to 1. At the extremes, the sine and triangle waveforms become ramp-down and ramp-up sawtooth waveforms, respectively. When sample-and-hold is activated, changing the width of the pulse waveform has a swing-like effect on the sample-and-hold step-sequence timing.

◆ The Randomizer Module sends out a random value whenever it receives a new event at its *In* input. The range of values is controlled by its *Rng* input, so use the context menu for that input to create a Range control. Although the pulse wave only takes two values per LFO cycle, these values are repeatedly sent to its output at Reaktor's Control Rate (Settings menu), which is typically several hundred times a second. (This will cause the sample-and-hold to change the oscillator pitch several hundred times a second—interesting, but not what we're after.) The Module with the ">>" icon is an Event-Merger (Auxiliary submenu) and it will eliminate these repeats. Create it and wire the LFO's *Pls* output through it and into the Randomizer's *In* input.

◆ For the output to the oscillator, we want to add the LFO signal to the sample-and-hold output. That way, with the LFO amount at zero, the output will be pure sample-and-hold whereas with the sample-and-hold switch turned off it will be pure LFO. Obviously, use an Event Add 2 Module cabled into the *O* output terminal for this.

◆ The remaining step is to set up the LFO output. Start with an Event Add 2 Module and a MIDI Controller Module (MIDI sub-menu) wired into its top input. Set up the MIDI Controller Module for MIDI Controller 1 (modulation wheel) and set its range to 0 to 1 and set its MIDI range 0 to 127.

▶ The MIDI range tells the MIDI Controller Module what range of MIDI values to convert to the Min/Max Range settings. We've set it to 0 to 127 because most Modulation controllers cover the full MIDI value range.

◆ Use the context menu for the Event Add 2 Module's second input to create an LFO amount control. Make it a medium size knob with range 0 to 10.

▶ Instead of multiplying the modulation amount, we could have used the MIDI Modulation Wheel to remote control the LFO amount knob, but that would not have allowed us to apply a fixed LFO amount.

◆ Multiply the output of the Event Add 2 Module by the LFO's *Sin* output (use an Event Mult 2 Module) and wire the output into the Event Add 2 Module feeding the *O* output.

◆ In the BS-5 Instrument Structure window, wire the *O* output of the LFO Macro into the Oscillator's *Pm* input. Open the Filter's Structure window and create an LFO input as shown in the illustration. In the BS-5 Instrument Structure window wire the *F* output into the Filter's LFO input. Rearrange the controls in the Instrument and Ensemble Control Panels and you're done.

◎ **29** BS-5 Sample & Hold and LFO

LFO input and amount control for modulating the filter cutoff frequency.

BS-6: Stereo Delay

The last enhancement to our basic synth is to add a stereo delay with cross-channel feedback. Instead of building it from scratch, however, we're going to *borrow* the delay Macro from the factory Ensemble, ManyMood. Behind the seeming complexity of its Structure (see illustration), lies a fairly straightforward design. Here is a brief rundown of how it works.

There are a pair of Static Delay Modules (1) whose delay times are set by a combination of *Coarse* and *Fine* knobs and a sine wave LFO (2) for a simulated chorus effect. The delay outputs, after optional inversion (3), are sent through a 1-Pole Filter Module (4) with both lowpass and highpass outputs. The highpass outputs are sent back to Mixer Modules for mixing both sides of the delay with the dry signal. The Mixer Modules actually supply the inputs to the Static Delay Modules. The Filters' lowpass outputs are wired into separate Crossfade Modules (5). The other inputs of the Crossfade Modules carry the dry signal. The result is a mix in each channel of the dry signal, the lowpass-filtered delay output and the highpass-filtered delay feedback from both channels. Note that there is also a switch (7) for taking the Macro completely out of the signal path and eliminating its CPU drain.

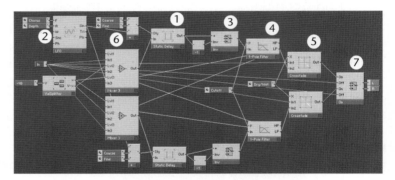

There are two ways to get the Stereo Delay Macro from the ManyMood Ensemble into our synth. The first is to simply load ManyMood, find and copy the Stereo Delay Macro, re-load BS-5 and paste the Macro into BS-5's Ensemble Structure. The other is to load ManyMood, find the Stereo Delay Macro and use its context-menu (right-click on the Macro) to save it to your hard drive. Then reload BS-5 and load the Stereo Delay Macro. The first method is quicker, but the second has the advantage that you then have the Stereo Delay Macro available whenever you want to add it to an Ensemble.

Once you choose one of these methods, all that's left to do is insert it between the filter and the output of our basic synth. Since the delay is stereo, you'll need to add a second Audio Output terminal and Audio Voice Combiner Module. Then insert the Stereo Delay Macro as shown in the illustration. Finally, in the Structure window, wire the right and left outputs from the Instrument into the *1* and *2* inputs of the Ensemble's Audio Output Module.

30   BS-6 Reverb

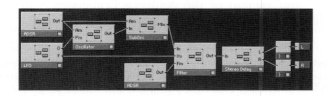

Instrument Structure window of the BS-6 Module with the Stereo Delay Macro inserted.

Odds and Ends

Before moving on to other synthesis methods, let's take a closer look at two things that are common to all Reaktor Ensembles: MIDI control and Snapshots.

MIDI Remote Control

In our previous discussions of Reaktor's Ensemble library, we've alluded to setting up and using MIDI Controller messages to automate Reaktor panel elements. The two obvious sources of these MIDI messages are a software sequencer running simultaneously and a hardware controller surface such as Native Instruments' 4Control.

Each panel element (i. e. knob, fader, switch, button or XY-control) has its own MIDI remote settings. The illustration shows the settings for a fader, but they are all similar. (Buttons have Trigger, Gate and Toggle modes. XY-controls have separate parameters for X and Y.)

There are two ways to implement MIDI remote control of a panel element:

♦ using Reaktor's MIDI Learn function activated from the Ensemble Toolbar,

♦ entering the settings manually in the MIDI section of the control's Properties window.

To use MIDI Learn, select the desired control, click the MIDI Learn Button and move the appropriate controller on your hardware controller surface. Reaktor will automatically set up the MIDI section of the control's Properties, which you may then wish to edit.

▶ A critical thing to remember is that an Instrument or Ensemble panel element will only respond to MIDI messages on the Instrument's or Ensemble's MIDI Channel. This also applies to the MIDI Learn function. An Instrument's or Ensemble's MIDI Channel can be set in its Properties window or in the Instrument Toolbar when the Instrument or Ensemble is selected.

Here are the details of the panel element MIDI properties:

♦ The Remote checkbox activates and de-activates MIDI remote control.

♦ The two output options—Panel to MIDI and Remote to MIDI—determine whether Reaktor sends the remote MIDI messages to its MIDI output when the control is changed on the panel or via incoming MIDI messages, respectively. Be aware that enabling Remote to MIDI can result in a MIDI feedback loop if the receiving device has a MIDI thru option that is enabled.

♦ Normally, incoming MIDI messages will be scaled to the panel element's range (set in the Range section) and the control will be set accordingly. If Soft Takeover is turned on, this will not happen until the incoming MIDI value matches the current control setting.

If Incremental is turned on, the incoming MIDI messages will be interpreted as indicating the hardware controller's direction and speed. (This only works with continuously rotating knobs such as those on Native Instrument's 4Control. In that case, incoming values of 64 and greater indicate clockwise motion with higher values indicating higher speeds. Similarly values of 63 and below indicate counterclockwise motion.)

Note that it makes no sense to turn both Incremental and Soft Takeover on. If Incremental is turned on, the Soft Takeover setting is ignored.

◆ Snap Isolate is not really a MIDI setting. It causes the control's value not to be stored and recalled with Snapshots.

◆ The Controller and Poly Aftertouch buttons are intended to allow either MIDI Controller or MIDI Poly Aftertouch messages to be used for MIDI remote control. However, the Poly Aftertouch option is not implemented at this time, so ensure that the Controller button is selected. Then use the Controller/Note No. box to select which MIDI Controller number is used.

▶ When MIDI Learn is used, Reaktor turns Remote on, tries (often successfully) to deduce whether to turn Incremental on or off and sets the MIDI Controller number. (Remember the incoming MIDI message must be on the correct MIDI Channel.)

Several panel-element MIDI-properties can be toggled globally from the Instrument or Ensemble Properties window. These include the incoming and outgoing MIDI Channel (they can be different), the Panel and Remote to MIDI Out properties and Incremental and Soft Takeover modes. When any of these properties is changed, the change applies to all controls on the Control Panel.

▶ There is one other global property called "Internal MIDI Routing". This allows MIDI to be routed between Control Panel controls within Reaktor. The routing can be between different Instruments or within the same Instrument. This allows you to slave one set of controls to another to, for example, control the levels of several Instruments with one control. Used with the MIDI Controller In and Controller Out Modules (see below), it also allows you to automate Control Panel controls from Reaktor processes (e. g. a step-sequencer or a Randomizer Module). A good example of this is the NewsCool Ensemble from the factory library (see "23 NewsCool" on page 71).

There are two other important Modules for affecting MIDI control: MIDI Controller In and MIDI Controller Out. Both are in the MIDI sub-menu of the Modules menu and they do just what their names imply—they receive and send MIDI Controller messages. Since Control Panel controls have built-in MIDI input and output capability, these Modules are only needed to communicate the output of Reaktor processing via MIDI.

The Properties of the MIDI Controller In Module are shown on the left with those of the MIDI Controller Out Module on the right. For incoming MIDI Controller messages, you set the Controller number, incoming value range (in case the external control does not use the full MIDI range) and the output range for the Module. Like a Control Panel control, the MIDI Controller In Module also has a Soft Takeover mode and

Snap Isolate feature. For the outgoing MIDI Controller messages, you set the Controller number and the range of values coming into the Module. This scales the range of values to the full MIDI data range of 0 to 127.

The MIDI Controller In Module is typically used to control some parameter for which there is no associated panel element. The MIDI Controller Out Module is used both to remote control external MIDI devices or other MIDI software and with Internal MIDI Routing, to affect Reaktor panel elements via other Reaktor processes. Chapter 7 "Handy Gadgets & Tricks" contains two examples: "Radio Buttons" on page 197 and "Control Randomizer" on page 200.

Snapshots Revisited

We had a brief look at Reaktor's Snapshot feature in Chapter 1 "First Light" (see "Snapshots" on page 15). Here we'll take a more detailed look at how to manage them.

The Ensemble and each Instrument has its own Snapshots. These can be saved to disk in banks of 128 and recalled by MIDI Program Change messages on the Instrument's or Ensemble's MIDI Channel. Thus, if an Ensemble's Instruments are assigned different MIDI Channels, their Snapshot can be recalled independently and conversely, if they are on the same MIDI Channel, their Snapshots will be linked. Instrument Snapshots can also be linked to the Ensemble's Snapshots and there are three crucial settings in the Ensemble and Instrument Properties that make this possible (see illustration):

Ensemble and Instrument Snapshot Properties.

◆ In order to recall Snapshots with MIDI Program Change messages, the Recall by MIDI checkbox must be checked.

(Although the other settings appear in the Ensemble's Properties, this is the only Snapshot setting that has any meaning for the Ensemble.)

◆ When an Instrument's Recall by Parent checkbox is checked, the Instrument's Snapshot will be automatically recalled whenever the Parent's Snapshot is. The thing to remember here is that it is the Snapshot *number* that the Instrument was set to when the Parent Snapshot was stored that is recalled. That is not necessarily the same number as the Parent's Snapshot.

◆ When an Instrument's Store by Parent checkbox is checked, the Instrument's settings will be automatically stored as a new Snapshot whenever the Ensemble's Snapshot is stored. If the Instrument is contained within another Instrument (called the "Parent"), its settings will also be automatically stored as a new Snapshot whenever a Snapshot is stored for the Parent.

▶ When Store by Parent is active, the Instrument Snapshot is stored before the Parent's so that when the Parent's Snapshot is recalled, it is the new Instrument Snapshot that is automatically recalled along with it.

Snapshot section of the Instrument Toolbar (top) and Snapshot window. The Snapshot button in the Toolbar (camera icon) opens the Snapshot window.

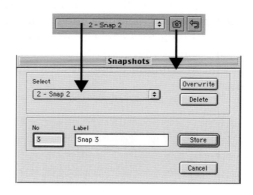

Snapshot management is handled through Reaktor's Snapshot window (see illustration). Here are some things to remember about managing Snapshots:

◆ The Snapshot window is opened by clicking the Snapshot button (camera icon) in the Instrument Toolbar. The Snapshot window applies to the selected Instrument or Ensemble. (That's why the button is in the Instrument Toolbar.)

◆ When you open the Snapshot window, Reaktor will suggest an unused Snapshot number and generic name. You can change either one, but if you select an already used number, the previous Snapshot with that number will be overwritten. (That can be useful and is also the only way to re-use the numbers of deleted Snapshots.)

◆ The Snapshot number is the same as the MIDI Program Number used to recall the Snapshot.

◆ The Snapshot menu in the Snapshot window is used for selecting Snapshots to be deleted or overwritten with the current Instrument settings. Using it does not recall the Snapshot (as using the same menu on the Instrument Toolbar does).

◆ To copy or rename a Snapshot, first recall it using the Instrument Toolbar; open the Snapshot window and type in a new name or number; then click the Store button.

Reaktor's Load and Save Snapshot dialogs. Once the Load or Save as ... buttons are clicked, standard file load and save dialogs appear.

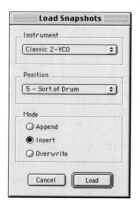

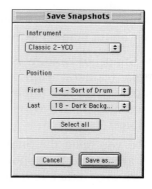

Disk management of Snapshots is handled via Reaktor's File menu. There are separate dialogs for loading and saving Snapshots. Any contiguous group of Snapshot can be saved. Loaded banks of Snapshots can be inserted at any point in the Snapshot list, appended at the end or overwrite existing Snapshots starting with any desired Snapshot. All these actions are subject to the 128 Snapshot limit per bank, however.

Here are a few final details on how Snapshots work:

◆ All Control Panel element settings are saved in a Snapshot.

◆ The settings of any MIDI Controller Module (input or output) used in the Instrument are saved in a Snapshot.

◆ Each Control Panel element has a unique Snapshot ID, which is visible and changeable in the element's Properties. Changing it will not update previously saved Snapshots, so do so at your own risk.

◆ Each Control Panel element has a Snapshot Isolate option in its Properties that will cause its settings not to be saved or recalled with Snapshot.

The last topic we'll cover in this section is Reaktor's Compare function. Every time you click the Compare button, Reaktor takes a temporary Snapshot of the Instrument's settings, then replaces those settings with the previously compared settings (if any). Once you change any setting, the just captured settings become the new basis for comparison. Using this function effectively is easier than it may sound:

1 Create or recall the settings with which you wish to start.

2 Click the Compare button. (If this is not the first time for this Instrument in this session, click the Compare button again.) The current settings are now your basis for comparison.

3 Tweak the Control Panel until you have a modification you want to compare with the original.

4 Click the Compare button as often as you like to toggle between the two. When you decide which one to keep, start tweaking again and Reaktor will automatically save it as the new basis for comparison.

Polyphony and the Dread Red X

In Chapter 1 we covered the often confused subjects of polyphony, multi-timbrality and audio channels (see "Voices, Channels and Outputs" on page 21). Now that we've done some wiring, let's look at polyphony again.

You can assign the number of voices allocated to an Instrument in its Properties or on the Instrument Toolbar. For Instruments with more than one voice, Reaktor keeps separate calculations going for each voice and will reveal the value for each voice when you mouse over its wires with Hints turned on.

Some Module inputs require that the data for the separate voices be combined. These include Audio In and Out Ports in Instruments (the same ports in Macros will accept separate voice data), displays such as meters and lamps, the inputs to the Ensemble Structure's Audio Out Module and any audio input to any Module or Macro that is restricted to mono operation.

▶ Modules and Macros have a Mono checkbox in their Properties, which, when checked, restricts them to mono operation.

If you try to wire an uncombined, polyphonic signal into these inputs, you get the red X indicating that the connection is not allowed.

The red X indicates that an uncombined polyphonic signal is wired into an input that requires a combined signal. The Voice Combiner Module combines the separate voices into a single signal.

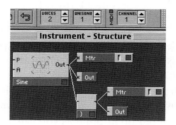

▶ The Voice Combiner does not affect polyphony, but it does eliminate the possibility of doing separate voice processing after its insertion into the signal path.

Here are some tips and tricks concerning monophonic operation and voice combining.

◆ Modules with built-in graphic displays—filters and envelopes, for example—show only one voice of a polyphonic signal. Therefore, you may not see parameter changes that vary from voice to voice (e. g. cutoff frequency tracking pitch).

▶ Many of the Instruments in this book are set to one voice for just that reason. In most cases they will also work polyphonically.

◆ If you want polyphonic effects processing you must keep the effect within the same Instrument as the signal it is processing. On the other hand, you can save lots of CPU by using monophonic effects.

◆ In some cases it is useful to set individual Modules to monophonic operation within a polyphonic Instrument. A monophonic LFO, for example, will modulate all targets in sync.

Variations on a Theme

In this section, we'll make some modifications to the basic synthesizers we constructed in the previous section. First we'll swap out our basic oscillator for a multi-waveform model with a little built-in oscilloscope. Then we'll add a second oscillator with hard-sync and we'll add a noise source.

▶ You'll find the synthesizers in this section—BSV-1 and BSV-2—in the Synthesizers folder inside the Ensembles folder on the WIZOO CD.

BSV-1: Multi-waveform Oscillators

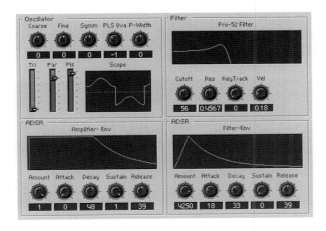

BSV-1 adds a multi-waveform oscillator and small oscilloscope to our basic synth.

This multi-waveform synth starts with our basic synth (see "BS-3: Using Macros" on page 88) and replaces its simple sawtooth oscillator with a multi-waveform oscillator with triangle, parabolic and variable-width pulse waveforms. There is no single Module for this, but we can easily combine two oscillator Modules to get the job done.

Recall that in BS-3, we wired the amplitude ADSR envelope Macro to directly control the oscillator's amplitude. Since we're now going to combine several oscillator signals using a Mixer Module, it's easiest to move the amplitude control to the end of the Structure.

In BSV-3, the amplitude ADSR is moved to the end of the Structure where it controls the output level by multiplying the audio output by the envelope amount.

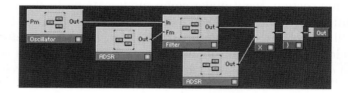

We mentioned earlier that there are many ways to control the amplitude of an audio signal. One of the simplest is to multiply the audio signal by the control signal (in this case the ADSR envelope output). This is what we've done in the BSV-1 Structure pictured above and we've used exactly the same ADSR envelope Macro as in BS-3. Now let's get to the oscillator.

Multi-waveform Structure. The outputs of a triangle/parabolic-wave oscillator and a pulse wave oscillator are mixed to produce complex waveforms.

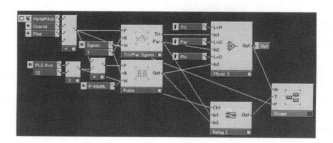

Here are the important points to notice about the multi-waveform oscillator structure:

◆ The pitch control section at the upper-left is the same as that used in BS-1 (see "BS-1: Oscillator and ADSR" on page 80).

- The pitch control section is wired directly into the *P* input of the Tri/Par Symm Module, but is added to an octave offset control before being sent to the *P* input of the Pulse Module. The octave divider control labeled *PLS 8va* steps in increments of one so that it will display the actual octave offset and its output is then multiplied by 12 so that each increment shifts the oscillator's pitch by 12 semitones.

- A symmetry knob (*Symm*) has been created for the Tri/Par oscillator and a pulse-width knob (*P-width*) has been created for the pulse wave oscillator. Having separate controls gives us a much broader range of combined waveforms.

- Both oscillators have their amplitudes set to 1—their levels are controlled at the Mixer Module. This points up another reason for moving the amplitude envelope to the end of the Structure—it allows separate control of the triangle and parabolic waveform levels.

- The Mixer Module (Mixer menu) has its level inputs calibrated in decibels. Typical control ranges for such inputs are –60 to 0 and this is the range chosen for the oscillator mix sliders. ◎ **31** BSV-1

The last thing to scope out in BSV-1 is the little oscilloscope in the new oscillator section. It is built around Reaktor's Scope Module. The Scope Module has an audio input for the audio signal to be analyzed, four event inputs for positioning and sizing the trace in the scope and a trigger input for synchronizing the trace to the waveform. The other modules synchronize the scope's tracking and graphic-scaling to the oscillator settings. Here's how they work:

The Structure view of the little oscilloscope built into the oscillator section of BSV-1.

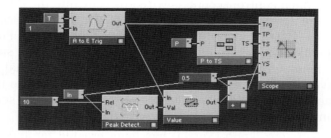

♦ The input to the scope comes from the output of the Mixer Module (i. e. it is the combined output of the three oscillators).

♦ The vertical scaling of the graphic (*YS* input) is controlled by a Peak Detector Module that calculates the peaks in the input signal and adds a slight offset. A new value is sent (via the Value Module) each time the scope is re-triggered.

♦ The trigger signal (*T* input) comes from the lower pitched of the two oscillators. That ensures that the scope retriggers once for each cycle of the mixed waveform. Each time a positive zero-crossing appears at the *C* input of the A to E Trig Module a value of 1 is sent to the Scope Module's *Trg* input, re-triggering the scope. The Relay 2 Module in the Oscillator Structure ensures that the output of the Pulse Module is used for the trigger if its octave offset is 0 or less and that the output of the Tri/Par Symm Module is used otherwise.

BSV-2: Sync'd Oscillators and Noise

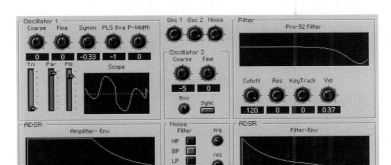

BSV-2 adds a second, sync'd oscillator and a noise generator to our basic synth.

In BSV-2 we've added a second, parabolic oscillator with a sync input and a noise generator with its own multi-mode filter and ADSR envelope. The three knobs at the top-center mix the outputs of the three sound sources before they are sent to the filter.

Some additional modulation possibilities have been added as well. For one, Oscillator 2 can be hard sync'd to Oscillator 1. For another, the noise generator's ADSR envelope can also be routed to modulate Oscillator 2's pitch. This is especially useful in combination with hard sync. Let's first take a look at the new oscillator.

The Structure of BSV-2 (top) and its Oscillator 2 (bottom). Oscillator 1 has been routed to hard sync Oscillator 2 and the Noise ADSR envelope has been routed to modulate Oscillator 2's pitch (black arrows).

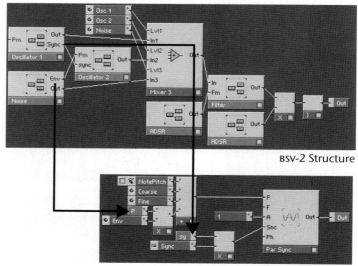

BSV-2 Structure

Oscillator 2

Oscillator 2's structure should look fairly familiar by now. Pitch is controlled by MIDI Note number, coarse and fine tuning knobs and a modulation input. (As mentioned this is wired to the new noise generator's ADSR envelope.) As with Oscillator 1, the amplitude is fixed at 1. The one new feature is hard synchronization via the Par Sync Module's *Snc* input.

▶ Hard synchronization means forcing one oscillator, the "slave", to restart its waveform whenever the waveform from another oscillator, the "master", crosses zero in the positive direction (i. e. when its value moves from negative to positive). If the master oscillator has a simple waveform such as a sine wave, there will be one positive zero-crossing per cycle and the slave oscillator will be synchronized to the pitch of the master. (If the slave oscillator is tuned to a different pitch than the master, then its waveform will be truncated, which will affect its timbre.) If the master oscillator's waveform is complex, there may be more than one positive zero-crossing per cycle, in which case the slave will be pitched to some harmonic of the master. Listen to Snapshots, "one zero" and "two zeros", for an example (and look at the scope).

One useful feature of hard synchronization is that changes in the sync'd oscillator's pitch will cause timbral changes while leaving its pitch unchanged. That is the reason for providing pitch modulation of Oscillator 2 by the ADSR envelope of the noise generator. That typically produces a vocal-like effect. For an example listen to the Snapshot, "Talk to Me".

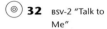

32 BSV-2 "Talk to Me"

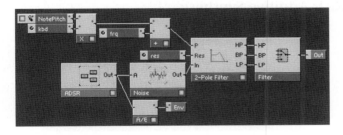

BSV-2 noise generator provides filtered noise and its own ADSR amplitude envelope.

The other addition to BSV-2 is the Noise Macro. The heart of its Structure is the Noise Module, which generates white noise. The Noise Module's only input is for controlling its amplitude and we've wired an ADSR envelope Macro in there. As mentioned, the ADSR envelope also has its own output which is wired to control Oscillator 2's pitch.

The Noise Module is followed by a 2-Pole Filter Module that has separate highpass, bandpass and lowpass outputs. An Audio Switch Module is used to select among them. The filter is resonant and has a pitch input. MIDI Note number is scaled by the *kbd* knob and added to the setting of the *frq* knob. If you select a bandpass filter and high resonance, you can use this as a pitched audio source as illustrated in the Snapshot, "Whistlin' Fifths". The fifths in this sound are produced by the Pro 52 filter, which is also set to high resonance and tuned a fifth above the noise tuning.

33 BSV-2 Whistlin' Fifths

Other Synthesis Methods

Now that we've run classical, subtractive synthesis into the ground, let's take a look at a couple of other common approaches.

▶ You'll find the synthesizers in this section—Add-1, FM-1, FM-2, WT-1 and WT-2—in the Synthesizers folder inside the Ensembles folder on the WIZOO CD.

Add-1: Additive Synthesis

Ensemble Control Panel for the 12 oscillator additive synthesizer, Add-1. The sine wave oscillators are organized in three groups of four. Each group shares a single ADSR envelope and is based on Reaktor's Multi-Sine Module, which provides four sine waves with independent tuning, level and output.

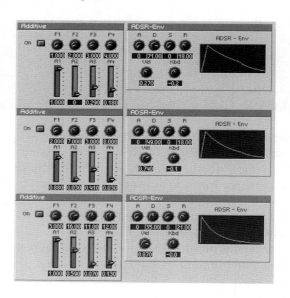

34 Add-1 Harmonic

35 Add-1 Inharmonic

Additive synthesis has been around since before there was synthesis—think organ. From a synthesis standpoint, it amounts to combining a number of sine wave oscillators at different frequencies and levels to construct complex waveforms.

You probably know—even if you're not sure exactly why—that any periodic waveform (which roughly speaking means any pitched sound) can be reconstructed from sine waves at harmonically related frequencies. (Harmonically related just means whole number multiples of the lowest frequency.) Of course, very interesting and clangorous things happen when you mix sine waves that are not harmonically related as well as when you change the mix during the course of the sound. In theory, you can reconstruct any sound this way, however, in practice, you can quickly run out of money and oscillators.

Our additive synth, Add-1, incorporates a couple of compromises aimed at reducing CPU load as well as the complexity of programming its sounds. For one thing, we've limited ourselves to 12 oscillators. This is barely enough for real additive synthesis, but the modular design makes it easy for you to add more if your CPU can handle it. (Even this modest system can max out a mid-level CPU at four to six voices.)

Our second compromise is in the dynamic mixing department. Dynamic mixing means changing the mix of the oscillators over time—obviously a job for an envelope generator. We've provided one ADSR envelope generator for each group of four oscillators. By carefully choosing the frequency relations of the oscillators within each group of four, you can produce a surprisingly complex dynamic mix. Also, you'll quickly come to appreciate only having to adjust ADSR parameters for three envelopes rather than 12.

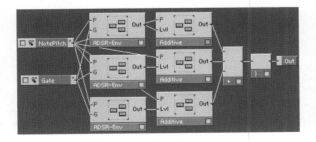

The Structure of the Add-1 Instrument. Each of the ADSR-Env and Additive oscillator Macros are identical. You can copy and paste to add more if your CPU can handle it.

You can see from the Instrument Structure that the ADSR envelope generators are providing control signals for the oscillator group levels. The MIDI Gate Module triggers the envelopes and the MIDI Note Pitch Module provides the oscillator pitches and also affects the ADSR-Env Macro's time settings. Here's how the time settings track the pitch (sometimes called keyboard tracking):

Macro Structure for providing pitch tracking of the envelope Attack, Decay and Release times.

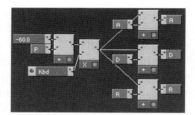

◆ 60 is subtracted from the incoming MIDI Note number, which means that the effect will be symmetric around Middle C. (I. e. there will be no effect at note number 60, which is Middle C.)

◆ The value of the *Kbd* knob is multiplied by the adjusted note number. The knob range is –1 to +1 so the effect can be positive or negative. (I. e. the times can get longer or shorter as the pitch rises.)

◆ The adjustment is added to the Attack, Decay and Release times.

Macro Structure for providing velocity-sensitive envelope amount.

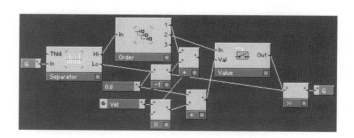

The process for providing velocity-sensitivity for the envelope amount is a bit more subtle. It works because the output of the ADSR-Env Module is scaled by the value of the gating signal. As we saw earlier, the Note Gate Module converts the note-on velocity to a value within its range, which we have set from zero to one. The rest of the circuitry scales the note-on velocity value by the setting of the *Vel* knob, whose range is also zero to one:

- The Separator Module splits the gate-on and gate-off signals. The gate-on goes through some processing starting with the Order Module, whereas the gate-off goes directly to the output via Event Merge Module (with the ">>" icon).

- The first output of the Order Module is used to scale the velocity and send it to the *Val* input of the Value Module.

- The second output of the Order Module is used to trigger the output from the Value Module. When any event arrives at its *In* input, whatever value is at its *Val* input is sent to the output.

▶ The Order Module is the only way to control the order in which events are propagated through the system.

- The rest of the Module's are there to restrict the velocity to between 0.80 to 1.00.

The Event Merge Module only passes signals when the value changes. Here it prevents multiple triggering of the envelope.

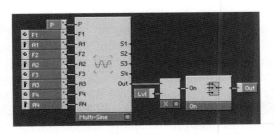

Add-1's oscillator Macros use Reaktor's Multi-Sine Module to mix four sine waves of different frequencies and amplitudes.

The only thing left is the oscillator groups, and their structure is very straightforward. They use a Multi-Sine Module, which provides four sine waves with their own frequency and amplitude settings. Separate outputs are also provided, but in this case we've used the combined output.

▶ If you want to envelope each sine wave individually, use the separate outputs.

The mixed output is multiplied by the Lvl input, which, you'll recall, is wired from the ADSR envelope output. The Switch Module at the end allows you to turn the oscillator group off to save CPU.

FM-1: Two-Operator FM Synth

Control Panel of FM-1, a basic, two-operator FM synth.

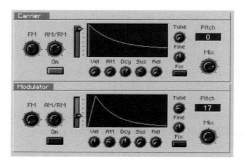

(◎) **36** FM-1

You could think of additive synthesis as making harmonically complex sounds the hard way—one sine wave at a time. There is a whole class of techniques collectively referred to as modulation synthesis (or sometimes, distortion synthesis) that produce complex harmonic structures using a small number of oscillators (sometimes only two). These include frequency modulation (FM), phase modulation (PM), amplitude modulation (AM) and ring modulation (RM). Each of these techniques uses one oscillator (called the modulator) to modulate (i. e. change) some parameter of another oscillator (called the carrier). In FM, the frequency is modulated, in PM the phase is modulated, and in AM and RM, the amplitude is modulated.

FM was made famous by the Yamaha corporation in its DX line of synthesizers from the Eighties. Actually those synths used PM, which produces nearly identical results, but has some technical advantages. Here we'll use FM because it's all that's available on Reaktor's oscillators. We'll also start with the simplest version—using one sine wave oscillator to modulate another. Other variations, which we'll have a look at in the next section, include using multiple oscillators with more complex modulation paths and using oscillators with complex waveforms.

When the modulator is in the low frequency range (think LFO), FM is called vibrato and AM is called tremolo.

All these modulation techniques have one thing in common—they produce complex waveforms from simple ones by adding new sine wave components (called "sidebands"). The frequencies of the sidebands are integer multiples of the modulator frequency added to the carrier frequency. (I. e. sidebands are produced on either side of the carrier frequency at distances which are multiples of the modulator frequency—hence the name "sideband".)

Modulation Technique	Sine Wave Frequencies	LFO
AM	$C-M$, C, $C+M$	Tremolo
RM	$C-M$, $C+M$	n/a
FM	... $C-2M$, $C-M$, C, $C+M$, $C+2M$ ...	Vibrato
C is the carrier frequency and M is the modulator frequency.		

The table shows the sine wave frequency components produced by AM, RM and FM. AM and RM produce only one pair of sidebands. They differ in that the carrier frequency is present in AM but not in RM. (We'll see how this is accomplished in a moment.) FM produces a lot more sidebands and their amplitudes are in a complex (not necessarily declining) relationship, which depends on the amount of modulation (also called the "modulation index"). The modulation index also controls the number of audible sidebands; generally more modulation means more sidebands. Before we get off

From the table you'll notice that in some circumstances the frequencies will be negative (e. g. when M or some multiple of M is bigger than C). That results in a component at the corresponding positive frequency (drop the "−" sign), but with inverted phase.

the technical bandwagon here are a couple of useful things to know:

▶ Digitally implemented FM can easily produce "aliasing" by generating sidebands at frequencies above half of the sampling rate (called the Nyquist frequency). These "fold over" around the sampling frequency (and consequently are less likely with higher sample rates) and produce alias frequencies. Since FM is about complexity and distortion, that is not always bad; it's just something to listen for.

Our basic FM synth uses identical "operators" for its carrier and modulator. It provides AM, RM and FM and even though simple, can produce some complex sounds. Here are the details:

Ensemble Structure of FM-1 (top) and the Macro Structure of its operators (bottom).

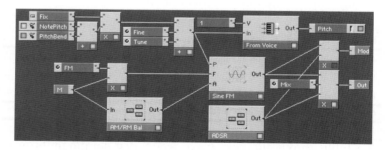

◆ The difference in the *Mod* and *Out* outputs is that the *Mod* output is not affected by the *Mix* knob. In more complex Structures, that allows you to control the output mix independently of the modulation amount.

◆ The Sine FM Module's *P* input, which is logarithmic, is used for tuning and MIDI keyboard control. Its *F* input, which is linear, is used for FM.

▶ Using the logarithmic *P* input for FM produces unevenly spaced side-bands (which can be an interesting effect) and also causes the pitch to change as the amount of modulation changes (almost always an undesirable effect).

◆ The *Fix* button cancels out the MIDI input. If you turn this on for the carrier and also set the tuning to zero (*Tune* knob full left and *Fine* knob centered), the carrier's frequency will be set to 0Hz. In reference to the table, that means that C = 0 and the sidebands will all be multiples of M. In other words, you will get complex, but harmonic waveforms (like a sawtooth with the levels of the harmonics all out of whack).

◆ The ADSR envelope is velocity sensitive and has its own amount control (the vertical slider at the left of the envelope graphic). It is applied to both the *Mod* and *Out* outputs and therefore provides both the mix and the modulation envelope. (We've seen enough envelopes now for you to dissect it on your own.)

◆ The purpose of the From Voice Module at the upper right of the Ensemble Structure is to ensure that the Control Panel Pitch display shows the carrier and modulator pitches for the same voice. It is displayed this way instead of showing the knob values directly because that takes into account the status of the *Fix* button. (There is no effect on the sound or function of the synth.)

◆ The AM/RM knob fades between AM (on the left) and RM (on the right). The practical difference between AM and RM is whether the modulating signal is bipolar (e. g. a sine wave oscillating between −1 and 1) or unipolar (e. g. a sine wave oscillating between 0 and 1). RM is just bipolar AM.

The AM/RM Bal Macro approximates this by adding an offset of one when the AM/RM knob is in the right half of its range. When the knob is in the left half of its range, no offset is added. In that case, since the modulating signal is bipolar, the result will be ring modulation. (We've cheated a little because, on the AM side, the signal is not necessarily unipolar—the amount of carrier in the mix varies with the amount of modulation.)

The use of the Not modules deserves some explaining. The purpose of the top one is to add an offset of one to the output when the *On* button is turned on and the AM/RM knob value is positive. The purpose of the bottom one is to generate a fixed output of one when the *On* button is turned off. That is necessary since the Macro is controlling volume—a zero output will silence the operator.

▶ The Not Module's *Out* output value is one when its input is greater than 0 and is zero otherwise.

Macro Structure for FM-1's AM/RM control, which fades between AM (left half of knob) and RM (right half of knob).

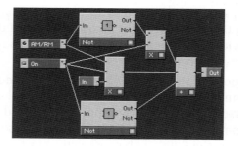

The operators in FM-1 are ideal for importing into other synths because they are self-contained, with controls for modulation amount, output mix, etc. You will find them implemented as a Macro and an Instrument in the Macros and Instruments folders on the WIZOO CD.

FM-2: Five-Operator Matrix-FM Synth

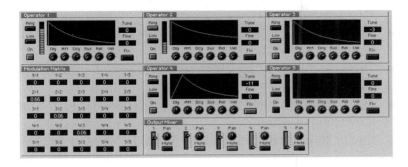

Control Panel of five-operator FM/RM synth, FM-2. The Modulation Matrix at the lower left controls modulation routings and amounts.

If you've ever had an FM synth, you know there's a lot more to FM than modulating one carrier with one modulator. FM-2 is an FM/RM hybrid offering five Operators and the ability to modulate any Operator by any other. Modulation is controlled via the five-by-five Modulation Matrix Macro at the bottom-left. You can scroll its numerical displays to create a broad range of modulation "algorithms". In addition, each Operator can be mixed into the output in any pan position using the small mixer at the bottom.

⊚ **37** FM-2

FM-2's Operators are essentially the same as FM-1's so we won't go into great detail, but here are the relevant differences:

◆ A delay with range 10 milliseconds to 5 seconds has been added to the envelope controls. You can use it for everything from delaying modulation by different operators to creating multi-taps. (If you want a different range, just double-click the control and enter your own values.)

◆ There are no envelope amount or mix controls. All Operators run at full tilt with the Modulation Matrix and Output Mixer controlling the levels.

◆ The Tune and Fine controls are numericals. Tune has a range of ±3 octaves in semitones and Fine has a range of ±0.5 semitones.

◆ The meter to the left of the envelope display shows the level of modulation.

◆ The *Ring* button toggles between ring (button on) and frequency modulation.

◆ The *Low* button reduces the modulation amount to 25% of the incoming amount.

◆ An *On* button has been added to each Operator (lower-left). Turning unused Operators off saves a lot of CPU.

FM-2's Modulation Matrix Structure. Each Operator is wired to an input and an output and the controls scale the inputs before mixing and routing to the outputs.

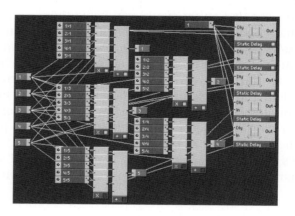

In spite of being densely packed, the Modulation Matrix is conceptually very simple. There are inputs and outputs for each Operator. Each input is multiplied by one of the numerical controls to scale its value from zero to one. Separate scaled inputs from each of the Operators are added up and sent to each of the outputs. The five numericals for a particular output control the mix of modulation going to the Operator wired to that output. The numericals are labeled on the Control Panel to indicate the source and destination.

This scheme allows each Operator to modulate itself (via the numerical controls on the diagonal running from top-left to bottom-right). Self-modulation is a handy FM trick, but it is more effective if the signal is delayed before being fed back. That's the point of the Delay Line Modules on the right.

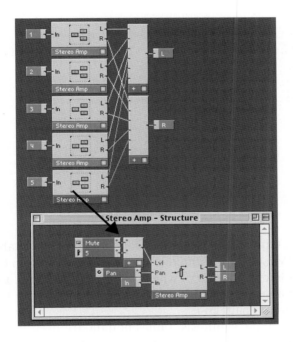

FM-2's Stereo Mixer Structure.

There are a lot of ways to make a mixer in Reaktor. In this case we've used the Stereo Amp Module (see inset), which makes life easy by supplying pan and level inputs. You can include any Operator in the final mix and pan it to any position. The *Mute* buttons are very convenient when setting up patches in FM-2.

Keep in mind that the mixer has no effect on the modulation routings.

Remember that we had keyboard scaling for the envelope times in the additive synth, Add-1 (see page 116).

A common feature of FM synths that we haven't included here is keyboard scaling of the FM amount. It is not hard to do, so give it a shot.

WT-1: Wavetable Synthesis

WT-1 Wavetable synth Ensemble Control Panel. WT-1 contains several preliminary Instruments. This is the final result—called Wave Grabber.

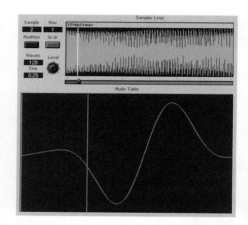

The last type of synthesis we'll take a look is wavetable synthesis. We saw an example of wavetable synthesis in Chapter 2 "The Factory Library" where we also introduced a simplified version of the synth we're going to build here (see "16 Virtuator" on page 57).

In wavetable synthesis, tables of data are used to describe waveforms. Reaktor's Audio Table Module is designed for exactly this and in order to understand what's going on, we'll start with a close look at how it works.

Not to belabor the obvious, but a table is just an arrangement of numbers in rows and columns (i. e. in two dimensions). The dimensions are usually referred to as "X" (horizontal) and "Y" (vertical). You can think of Y as indicating the row number and X as indicating the position or "cell" within the row. In wavetable synthesis, the values in the cells can be thought of as sample values and in this sense, each row can be thought of as a waveform—i. e. the waveform that would result from looping the sample values in that row.

▶ When we talk about a "waveform" in a wavetable we will always mean the waveform that results from looping the data in one row of the table.

Before building the complete wavetable synth, WT-1, let's look at some examples that illustrate how the Audio Table Module works. These are all contained in Instruments in the WT-1 Ensemble in the Synthesizers folder inside the Ensembles folder on the WIZOO CD. First let's set up a simple table and see how to manually read its values.

Structure for manual lookup in first
row of table

Processing Properties

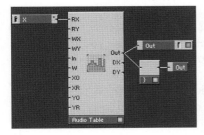

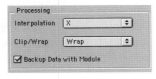

Numerical Properties

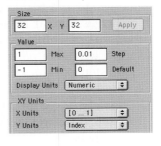

How Reaktor's Audio Table Module really works.

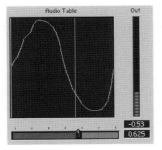

Audio Table graphic display with slider for selecting position and meter for displaying table value at selected position

The Audio Table Module has numerous inputs and outputs, but all that is necessary to play a single waveform (remember that means a row of the table) are the *RX* input for selecting cells in the row and the *Out* output for playing the values from those cells. In this example, we've wired a slider into *RX* to select the cells and wired a meter to the output to display the values. (We've also wired the output to an Audio Out Terminal and, in the Ensemble Structure, wired that to Reaktor's Audio Out Module. That is necessary to activate the Modules and, eventually, to hear the results.)

The Audio Table Module has several pages in its Properties, but the main one for setting it up is the Table page shown at the lower-right of the illustration. The Size boxes set the number of rows (Y) and the number of cells in each row (X).

▶ If you're thinking in terms of a table, the number of cells is the same as the number of columns.

Our table has 32 rows with 32 cells in each row. That means that each waveform has 32 values. Normally, you'd use more cells for better resolution, but 32 serves our purposes for now.

Once you've set up the table sizes, you need to set up the value range and resolution. For audio, this is typically −1 to 1, which is similar to setting an oscillator's *A* input to 1. A waveform reaching the upper and lower boundaries of the window will be bi-polar with an amplitude of 1.

The Step parameter sets the waveform's resolution—you can think of it as a kind of quantization. If we had set it to "1", for example, the only values allowed would have been −1, 0 and 1 and we could only draw in pulse waves. The Default value is the value that is automatically placed in all cells when they are created. Zero is a good choice because it ensures there is no DC offset generated by cells whose values you haven't changed.

The XY Units section is very important, but can seem a little confusing at first. Once you've set up the table's dimensions and what values are allowed in the cells, you still need a way of selecting individual cells because that is how you send their values to the output. The *RY* input is used for selecting the row (i. e. waveform) and the *RX* input, for selecting the cell.

The XY Units section allows you to specify how those selections are made. "Index" means just use the row or column number and this is the typical choice for Y Units.

▶ The rows are numbered starting at zero and if nothing is wired to the RY input, row zero is selected by default.

[0...1] means that whatever the number of cells is (i. e. the X or Y size) they are accessed using numbers between zero and one. In the case of 32 cells, for example, the cell selection changes in increments of $\frac{1}{32}$ (0.03125). [0...1] is a natural choice for an Audio Table Module because, as we'll see, it makes it easy to use an oscillator to scan through the table.

You may be wondering what happens when the inputs at RX and RY are not in the units specified. Good question and Reaktor has a clever answer, which is in the Processing of the Properties' Function page. The Interpolation menu controls what happens for "in-between" values and the Clip/Wrap menu controls what happens beyond the range limits.

Interpolation can be set to None, X, Y or XY. When set to None, the value in the closest cell to the selection number is taken. Think of it as quantizing. (In fact, try turning it on in the slider example and you'll see the waveform become quantized.) If any other Interpolation setting is used, Reaktor scales the values for intermediate indices relative to values in adjacent cells. Notice that this can be turned on independently for X and Y.

When the Clip/Wrap parameter is set to "Clip", *RX* and *RY* values beyond the table range will cause the value of the last cell to be output. When "Wrap" is selected, values beyond the table range will cause Reaktor to wrap around to the beginning of the table.

Although the Audio Table Module is connected to Reaktor's audio output, you're unlikely to have heard anything beyond a few clicks and pops unless you've been able to wiggle the slider very fast (as in 20 to 30 times a second). To cycle through a waveform in the Audio Table Module at audio rates, we need something to update its *RX* input at audio rates. Specifically, we need the RX value to go in a straight line from zero to one at the frequency corresponding to the desired pitch. A Ramp Module is the best choice.

Instrument Control Panel and Structure for playing waveforms from the Audio Table Module. The oscilloscope at the right shows that the output waveform matches the waveform in the selected row of the Audio Table Module. A Ramp Module whose output runs from zero to one is used to scan the waveform at the desired pitch.

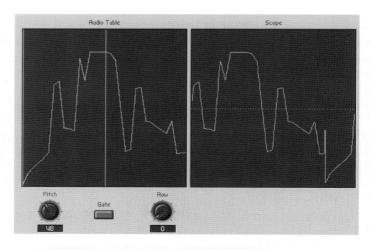

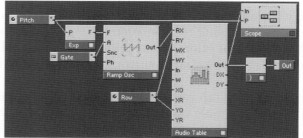

The only things you need to notice about this structure for playing the Audio Table Module's waveforms are the conversion of the *Pitch* knob to frequency for setting the Ramp's *F* input and the addition of the *Row* knob to select which waveform row is selected. The *Row* knob runs from 0 to 31 in steps of one and it is also wired to the *YO* input so that the Audio Table Module's display will show the selected row.

The *Gate* button toggles between 0 and 1, which causes the Ramp Module's output to run from 0 to 1—just what we want for the *RX* input.

▶ Notice that the range matches the X-Units setting in the Audio Table's Properties. Alternately, we could have set that to "index" and used a gate value equal to the Audio Table's X-size. The advantage of our method is that you can change the X-size without having to adjust the gate value.

This is a good time to see how waveforms are created in the Audio Table Module. The simplest method is drawing with the mouse. With the *Gate* button on, select different rows of the Audio Table and click-drag with the mouse inside the graphic display. When you're over that, right-click (⟨ctrl⟩-click on the Mac) in the graphic display and choose "Select Mode" from the Process sub-menu of the context menu. Now click-drag again in the graphic display and you'll see that a section of the waveform turns gray indicating that it is selected. You can use the Process section of the context-menu to modify the waveform in various ways.

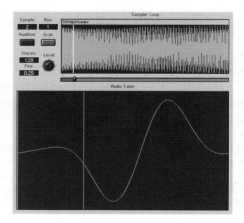

Instrument Control Panel for capturing waveforms from samples. The horizontal slider selects the position in the sample and the *Loop* knob sets the loop length. When the *Grab* button is on, the sample loop is being captured in the selected row of the Audio Table.

Two other alternatives are to load and save audio tables from your hard drive and to capture them in real-time from other audio sources. The first is straightforward, so we'll move on to real-time scanning next.

Our waveform source will be Reaktor's Sampler Loop Module, which allows you to loop any portion of any sample in its memory. When the Sampler Loop Module's Oscil. Mode is turned on, it treats the selected loop as a waveform and plays it back (i. e. oscillates it) at the desired pitch.

▶ Samples (called wavesets) made up of a series of individual waveforms make good sources for waveform capturing. A number of these are provided on the Reaktor CD.

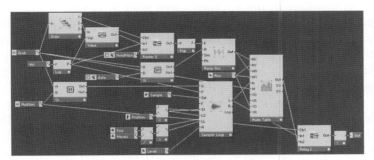

Full Structure

Instrument Structure for capturing waveforms from samples. The full version (top) adds MIDI playback and auditioning of the sample both of which require extra Modules to handle the logic. The simplified version (bottom) contains everything necessary to capture the sample loops.

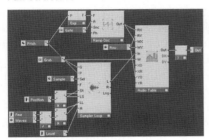

Simplified Structure

In order to capture a waveform in the Audio Table Module we need to playback the waveform into the Audio Table Module's *In* input and tell the Audio Table Module where and at what rate to store the incoming sample values. The *WY* input is for selecting the row to be written into and we have wired the row selector numerical into it so that the same row is being read, written and displayed. The *WX* input is for selecting the cells to be written into and we have wired the ramp that reads the waveform (i. e. that is wired into the *RX* input) into the *WX* input. Finally, we have to tell the Audio Table Module when to write values into the table and this is what the *W* input is for. We've wired the *Grab* switch into it and also into the *G* input of the Sampler Loop Module to simultaneously start it playing.

As mentioned, the Sampler Loop Module is specifically designed for looping segments of a sample as an oscillator waveform. Its *St* and *LS* inputs set the location of the start of the loop. (They both need to be connected in order for playback to start at the start of the loop when the sample is triggered.) The LL input sets the length of the loop.

We've used a little slight-of-hand in setting up the loop-length controls. The Sampler Loop Module's *Lng* output tells the length (in ms) of the selected sample. That length is divided by the value of the *Waves* numerical and the *Fine* numerical then scales the result by a value between zero and one. This is handy if you're using a waveset sample and know how many waves are in the waveset. In that case, set the *Waves* numerical to the number of waves in the waveset and set the *Fine* numerical to one. When you're not using a waveset sample, use the *Waves* numerical as a coarse control and then fine tune it with the *Fine* numerical.

Everything described so far is incorporated in the simplified version of the Structure shown in the illustration. In the full version we've added a few bells and whistles that will make the Wave Grabber Instrument useful in our next synth (see "WT-2: Vectored Wavetable Synthesis" on page 137):

◆ You can audition the Sampler Loop Module's playback (i. e. the current loop) by using the *Audition* button.

◆ You can play the Audio Table Module from a MIDI keyboard when the *Grab* button is turned off.

◆ The pitch when grabbing a waveform or auditioning the Sampler Loop Module's output is fixed at 441Hz. At that frequency, one wave cycle contains 100 samples when Reaktor's sample rate is set at 44,100Hz. The Audio Table Module's X-size has accordingly been set to 100.

▶ A note about grabbing: you'll notice that WT-1 is set to one voice. Grabbing waveforms works much better in this mode (try the alternative and you'll see why). But once your wavetable is full, WT-1 works well as a polyphonic synth, too.

▶ Another note about grabbing: when you grab a waveform, you may get occasional spikes. You can always grab again, but these are also easily smoothed out with the mouse.

WT-2: Vectored Wavetable Synthesis

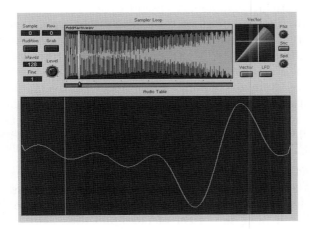

Ensemble Control Panel of the vector synth WT-2.

Now that we know how to capture and play wavetables, let's add a little motion to the picture. A lot of techniques involving wavetables go under the name of vector synthesis, but they all have one thing in common: they provide control of the path through the wavetable.

In WT-1, we used a Ramp Module to "scan" a row of the Audio Table Module in order to playback the waveform in that row and we used a numerical control to select which row. But once we have a table full of waveforms, there's no reason to restrict ourselves to one-dimensional scanning. If, for example, we wire the Ramp Module into both the RX and RY inputs of the Audio Table Module, the resulting path (a. k. a. vector) will be the diagonal from bottom-left to top-right of the audio table.

For more variety, we could scale the Ramp Module by different amounts for the horizontal and vertical dimensions.

○ **38**   WT-2 Manual
Vectoring

That would create different upward-slanting, vectors through the audio table. Our next wavetable synth, WT-2, provides this and more.

WT-2 adds an XY Module to WT-1 for controlling the wavetable vector. The *Vector* button turns vector synthesis on and off; when turned off, WT-2 works just like WT-1. When vectoring is on, the vector can be controlled either directly with the XY Module or dynamically using dual LFOs. In LFO mode (when the LFO button is on), the XY Module controls the frequencies of the two LFOs.

The XY Module acts both as a controller and a display. The blue oscilloscope-like trace displays the current vector.

▶ If you think of the XY Module's display as representing the wavetable, then the oscilloscope trace corresponds to the path through the table.

In direct mode (LFO off) the vector is fixed and runs from the bottom-left of the table to the intersection of the cross-hairs. If you hold a note in direct mode while moving the cross-hairs you'll hear the effect of changing the vector while a note is sounding. The LFOs automate this process.

WT-2 Instrument Structure. The Modules from WT-1 making up the sampler and ramp-scanner sections have been incorporated into Macros.

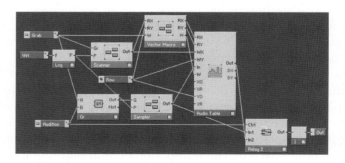

Our starting point for WT-2 is WT-1, but we have cleaned things up a bit, by encapsulating the sampler and ramp-scanner sections in Macros. The only real addition is the Vector Macro. Note that the ramp-scanner and Row numerical are both wired into the Vector Macro instead of directly into the *RX* and *RY* inputs of the Audio Table Module. That allows us to switch between vectoring and normal operation.

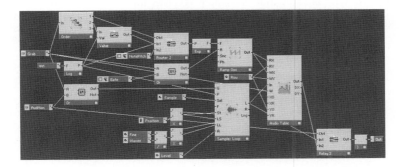

Vector Macro Structure of WT-2.

Before you freak out, notice that four of the Modules in this Structure are just switches (two Event Routers, two Audio Relays) and six of the Modules are terminals. The rest is pretty simple. The Audio Relays switch the output between the direct *RX* and *RY* inputs (WT-1 mode) and vector processing. The Vector processing simply amounts to multiplying the *RX* input (remember that is the ramp-scanner output) by separate values. The Event Routers switch the multipliers between the direct output of the XY Module and the output of the LFO Macro. (The Smoother Modules—with the "S" labels—smooth the output of the XY Module so that when you move the vector by hand, the transition between sounds is smooth.)

The last piece of the puzzle is the dual-LFO used for changing the vector in real time. It uses the sine wave output of two LFO Modules with amplitude and offset adjusted to produce an output range of zero to one. Their frequency is controlled by the XY Module via the *MX* and *MY* inputs and the incoming values are multiplied by the *Spd* knob. When the *Snc* button is turned on, MIDI gate signals are transferred (via the And Module) to the LFO's *Snc* inputs, which causes the LFO cycles to reset with each MIDI gate. Finally, the *Phz* knob

◎ **39** WF-2
Synchronized LFO vectoring

controls the phase at which the LFOs are reset when sync is on.

◎ **40** WF-2 Free running LFO vectoring

▶ LFO sync ensures that each note receives the same vector modulation—a good idea for lead sounds. Turning LFO sync off leaves the LFOS free running, which is often desirable for polyphonic pads and ambient sounds.

Vector LFO Macro Structure.

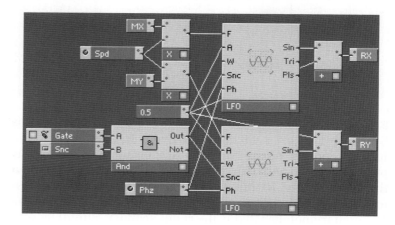

▶ Keep in mind that you need to fill all 32 rows of the Audio Table Module with waveforms to get the full effect of vectoring. Grabbing makes this easy—just turn the *Grab* button on and change rows and positions of the horizontal slider until you've filled the table with waveforms.

As with WT-1, grabbing waveforms works best when WT-2 is set to one voice.

One thing you'll notice about WT-2 is that there are no envelopes or filters. You can eliminate clicks and pops by adding an AR envelope and letting the Ramp Module run continuously and when LFO vectoring is on, the output could benefit from some high-shelving. You'll find both enhancements in the Ensemble, WT-2+. Try adding some effects.

4 Building a Sampler

In this chapter we'll build some sample players using Reaktor's eight different sample player Modules. Each of those Modules has its own feature-set designed for a particular kind of application. Two Modules—Beat Loop and Sampler Loop—facilitate playback and management of loop samples. Three others—Sample Resynth, Sample Pitch Former and Grain Cloud—are based on granular resynthesis techniques that allow independent pitch, time and formant manipulation. Then there are a couple of bread-and-butter samplers—Sampler and Sampler FM—and an odd duck named "Sample Lookup" that allows you to jump around randomly within the sample while it is playing. We've seen some of these sample player Modules in action the previous two chapters. Now we'll get into the specifics.

Building a Very Simple Sampler

As in Chapter 3 "Building a Synthesizer", we'll start with the simplest possible sampler and build up from there. But we won't go back to the step-by-step details that began that chapter, on the assumption that we've all had enough of that by now.

▶ You'll find the samplers in this section—vss-1, vss-2 and vss-3—in the Samplers folder inside the Ensembles folder on the WIZOO CD.

VSS-1: Basic Sampler

Ensemble Control
Panel and Structure
for the basic sampler
VSS-1.

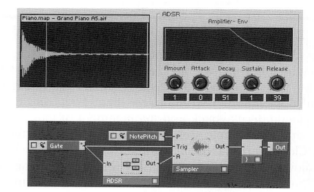

Our first very simple sampler, VSS-1, is about as basic as it
gets. It uses Reaktor's simplest sampler Module, appropri-
ately named "Sampler". Sampler has inputs for pitch (*P*), amplitude (*A*) and triggering the sample (*Trig*). The ADSR Macro
is our old friend from the previous chapter and MIDI Note
Pitch and Gate Modules are used to control Sampler's pitch
and triggering as well as gating the ADSR envelope.

▶ If you're wondering why the Sampler Module has a trigger rather
than a gate input, that is because the Sampler and Sampler FM Modules always play samples all the way through when triggered. Furthermore, if looping is turned on (see below) the loop continues to
play until a new trigger is received. It is up to you to control the enveloping of the sound.

The instructive value of VSS-1 is in seeing how Reaktor's sampler Modules work. Like all other Reaktor Modules, each
sampler Module has a Properties window and with the samplers, that is where all the action is. Reaktor's keyboard
mapping is rather primitive by today's standards—for example, there are no velocity zones and there is no graphic editor
for keyboard mapping—but there are also some unique features that give you lots of flexibility in building your own

sampler Ensembles. One is Oscil. Mode, which we've had a good look at in the wavetable synths WT-1 and WT-2 (see "WT-2: Vectored Wavetable Synthesis" on page 137). Another is the way looping is handled, which we'll have a look at in the next section (see "Looping Based Samplers" on page 150).

Sample Map I/O

Sample Map display.
Select individual samples here for setting their properties.

Individual Sample I/O

Sample MIDI note mapping

Looping properties

Playback properties

The Properties window for the Sampler Module is the nucleus for the Properties of all other sampler Modules. The top section is for loading and saving sample Maps as well as adding samples to them. You can drag-and-drop samples into the scroll-window as well as importing AKAI format sample Maps. WAVE, AIFF and SDII sample formats are supported. Once you have some samples in the Map, you select them individually to set their properties and you can also perform some remedial disk operations on the selected samples (i. e. replace or reload them).

All samples used by Reaktor samplers are held in RAM, but sample management is smart enough not to reload the same sample when it is used in another Module. On the other hand you can choose to save samples along with the Ensemble—click the "Backup Sound" checkbox to do so. In that case, Reaktor will attempt to reload the original sample when the Ensemble is reopened, but failing that, it will use the stored version. (That's the meaning of the "restored" indication next to the samples in the illustration.) The point is that for re-stored samples Reaktor does not know that they are dupli-cates of other samples in use.

▶ Saving samples with your Ensembles makes your Ensembles large, takes up extra disk memory and can lead to inefficient use of RAM. It's a good idea not to do it unless the Ensemble will be separated from the samples it uses (e. g. if you want to distribute the Ensemble with-out the individual samples).

The Sampler Properties' Left Split, Root Key and Detune fields should be familiar if you've ever seen a sampler before. The Left Split is the lowest MIDI Note Number that will play that sample. The Root Key is the MIDI Note Number that will play the sample at its natural rate. (Root Key doesn't apply in Oscil. Mode.) Detune allows you to fine tune your samples in cents ($1/100$'s of a semitone).

▶ Keep in mind that the highest MIDI Note Number that plays a particu-lar sample is one less than the Left Split of the next sample in the Map. So, if you load a single sample into the Map and set its Left Split to zero, the whole MIDI keyboard will play the sample.

The Properties in the Loop section control how samples are played back and there are more choices for the more com-plex sampler Modules. The On/Off checkbox tells Reaktor whether to loop the sample during playback. If there is a loop defined within the sample, Reaktor will use it. Other-wise Reaktor will loop the whole sample. You can't define your own loops, but Reaktor's loop-oriented sampler Modules provide a better alternative (more later).

The Alternating Loop checkbox controls whether Reaktor jumps back to the beginning at the end of the loop or reverses playback direction until reaching the beginning again. The latter is often smoother for the sustain portion of instrument and vocal samples. Backward and Forward are not really loop parameters—they control whether the whole sample is played forward or backward.

▶ Note that the settings in the Loop section apply to the individual selected sample in the Map. If you want to make a particular setting (turning looping on for example) for all samples click the "Apply to all Samples in Map" button. But bear in mind, that applies to all settings in the Loop section.

We've discussed the Oscil. Mode and Backup Sound options already. As with all Modules, Mono restricts the Module to one-voice and Mute silences it altogether, which is very handy for debugging your Ensembles.

The Quality section of the Properties controls how Reaktor interpolates between sample values during playback. Choosing "Poor" results in no interpolation. The better Quality settings take more calculation. Keep in mind that low quality does not necessarily mean "bad".

An obvious question at this point is: "what about sampling?" Well, Reaktor's samplers don't sample, they only play samples. When you want to sample the output of an Instrument or the input from an external source, you use the built-in Audio Recorder (see "Audio File Recorder and Player" on page 23) or one of Reaktor's Tape Deck Modules.

vss-2: Waveforms and Oscil. Mode

Ensemble Control Panel and Structure of vss-2 sample wave-player.

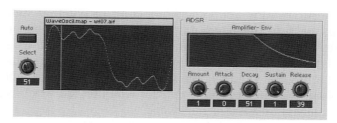

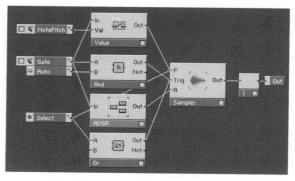

⊚ **41**   vss-2

vss-2 illustrates how to use the Sampler Module as a wave-player. The Oscil. Mode property is turned on for each of the samples in the Map, which means that the samples will be looped at the rate necessary to produce the pitch at the P input rather than at the rate dictated by their Root Key. (Notice that the Root Key option is no longer available in the Properties.) In essence, each sample is treated as if it were an oscillator waveform. Oscil. Mode is usually most effective when the samples in the Map are single-cycle waveforms as they all are in the Map used in vss-2.

In vss-1 we used the incoming MIDI Note Number to both select the sample from the map and control the playback pitch. Those processes can be separated and one often wants to do so when using waveform samples in Oscil. Mode. In that case, the sample selection controls the timbre while the MIDI Note Number controls the pitch.

vss-2 uses some logic circuitry to offer both alternatives. The trick involved is that the selected sample will not change until the Sampler Module is re-triggered. The *Select* knob always sets the pitch and selects the sample because the bottom Or Module ensures that a new trigger is sent each time the knob changes value. On the other hand, while a new MIDI Note Number always goes to the *P* input, its corresponding MIDI Gate does not re-trigger the Sampler Module unless the *Auto* button is turned on. (That's the purpose of the And Module.) So, with *Auto* turned off, you can play the selected waveform over the whole MIDI keyboard range.

▶ Notice that the *P* and *Trig* inputs of the Sampler Module each have two wires going into them. You can do this with Event inputs and the most recently changed value will be the one used. (You can not do this with Audio inputs, however.)

VSS-3: FM and Oscil. Mode

VSS-3 replaces the oscillators of a two-operator FM synth with FM sample players.

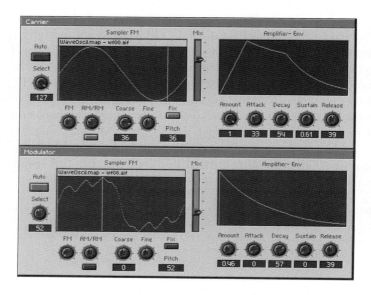

 42   VSS-3

You could use a Sampler Module in Oscil. Mode to replace any of the oscillators in the synths of Chapter 3, which means you can combine sampled waveforms with other oscillators and sound generators and apply filtering and other processing. But when it comes to modulation techniques other than simple AM, you're out of luck. Of course, Reaktor provides an answer and that is the Sampler FM Module.

Sampler FM is the Sampler Module with a couple of extra inputs: one for FM and one for setting the start-point in the sample for re-triggering. We'll take advantage of the FM input to replace the FM oscillators in our basic FM synth (see "FM-1: Two-Operator FM Synth" on page 120) with samplers. Using complex waveforms (instead of sine waves) to frequency modulate each other results in much more complex harmonic spectra and two operators are usually enough.

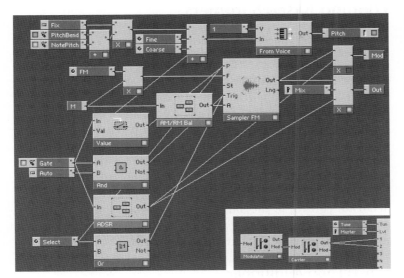

Instrument Structure for VSS-3's Carrier and Modulator Instruments. The Ensemble Structure is inset at the lower-right.

Starting with the RM/FM Operator Instrument from FM-1 (see page 122) it's simple surgery to plug in the Sampler FM Module in place of the Sine FM Module. But we also want the circuitry for select and auto-select of samples from VSS-2 (see page 146). We've pasted that as well. Here are the two necessary modifications to the original Structure:

◆ Originally, the output of the Event Add3 Module at the top-center of the illustration was wired directly into the Sine FM Module's *P* input. Now it has been wired into the *Val* input of the Value Module, which along with the *Select* knob controls the pitch of the Sampler FM Module.

◆ The ADSR Macro from VSS-2 replaces the ADSR Macro in the original FM-1. That just makes its gate external because we're using the gate for other purposes as well. (That change is not absolutely necessary—you could use two Gate Modules instead.)

Looping Based Samplers

▶ You'll find the samplers in this section—SLp-1, SLp-2 and SLp-3—in the Samplers folder inside the Ensembles folder on the WIZOO CD.

Reaktor has three sampler Modules that are ideal for manipulating long, looping sound files like beat-loops and speech fragments. The simplest, Sampler Loop, allows you to control the playback start-point (i. e. the position where the sample begins to play when it is gated), the loop start-point and the loop length. The Beat Loop Module adds automatic tempo calculation to facilitate breaking the loop into logical segments. Finally, the Sample Lookup Module gives you sample-accurate control of the sample pointer—you could think of it as the sampler equivalent of the Audio Table Module that we used in the wavetable synths in Chapter 3.

SLp-1: Loop Auditioner

SLp-1 offers manual control of all sample looping parameters.

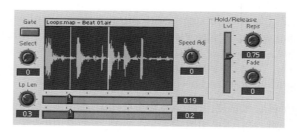

◎ **43** SLp-1

SLp-1 is primarily for auditioning loops to find good start and loop points, but it is also a fairly flexible loop player. Playback can be gated by the *Gate* button or MIDI Gates. In the latter case, the *Reps* knob determines how long playback continues (i. e. the envelope hold time)—it is calibrated in fractions of the sample length. The *Fade* knob controls the fade-out time (i. e. the envelope release time) also in fractions of the sample length. Use the *Select* knob to select the desired loop from the sample Map, then use the *St*, *LS* and *LL* sliders to adjust the loop to taste.

The Sampler Loop Module works slightly differently than the samplers we've used so far. For one thing it is gated rather than triggered; playback loops as long as the gate (e. g. MIDI note) is held, but stops as soon as it is released. There is an override for this in the Sampler Loop Module's Properties called "Loop in Release". When that is turned on, the gate input works like a trigger—i. e. the sample plays continuously as with the Sampler and Sampler FM Modules.

The Sampler Loop Module has separate inputs for pitch (*P*) and sample select (*Sel*), but you can still use pitch to select samples by leaving the *Sel* input un-wired. There is also a linear frequency input (*F*) that is handy for speed adjustments independent of sample selection.

Finally, there are three inputs and one output tailored specifically to loop management. The inputs (*St*, *LS* and *LL*) set the playback start-point when the Sampler Loop Module is gated and set the loop start-point and length. The output (*Lng*) tells the length of the selected sample in milliseconds. As we'll see, that is handy when you want to set the other parameters as fractions of the full sample length.

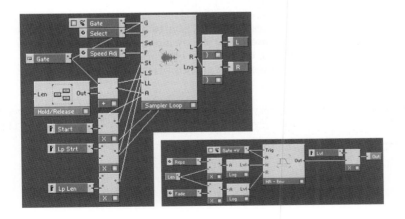

Instrument Structure of SLp-1. The start, loop-start, loop-length and hold time are all set as fractions of the sample length. The inset shows the hold-release envelope structure.

The Sampler Loop Module in SLp-1 is set up to play back longer sound files such as percussion loops or speech fragments rather than waveforms or instrument samples. It's sample Map assigns the samples consecutive Left Split keys starting at zero and assigns the Root Key to be the same as the Left Split. Therefore, a number at the *P* input both selects the sample assigned to the corresponding Left Split and plays it at its natural rate. The *Speed Adj* knob adjusts the loop playback speed in a range of ±5Hz.

The *Start*, *Lp Strt* and *Lp Len* sliders all run from zero to one and have their value multiplied by the *Lng* output value before being wired to the *St*, *LS* and *LL* inputs. That allows those parameters to be set as the same fraction of the full loop length, no matter which sample is selected.

SLp-1 playback is gated either by the *Gate* button or by MIDI Gate via the Hold/Release Macro. If the *Gate* button is used, the playback continues as long as the button is on so that you can audition other parameter changes. If MIDI Gate is used, the HR-Env Module controls the amplitude of the Sampler Loop Module. Both its hold and release times are set as a fraction of the sample length. (The purpose of the Log Modules is to convert milliseconds into the $^{dB}/_{ms}$ calibration of the HR-Env Module's *H* and *R* inputs.)

▶ $^{dB}/_{ms}$ is a logarithmic scale in which zero corresponds to one millisecond and each increase of 20$^{dB}/_{ms}$ multiplies the time by 10. (I.e. 20 = 10ms, 40 = 100ms, 60 = 1000ms, etc. For more on converting values scales in Reaktor see "Units and Conversions" on page 208.)

SLp-2: Beat Loops

Instrument Control Panel of SLp-2 beat loop player.

As its Control Panel suggests, SLp-2 is almost identical to SLp-1. However, it uses Reaktor's Beat Loop Module, which allows it to be synchronized to MIDI clock and provides independent control of playback pitch and speed. It accomplishes this neat trick by assuming that the sample has an exact power of 2 number of beats (e.g. 2, 4, 8, 16, 32, etc.), then using the sample length in milliseconds to calculate its tempo in the range of 87 to 174BPM.

⊚ **44** SLp-2

▶ For example, if the sample is exactly eight seconds long, the Beat Loop Module will assume it is 16 beats long at 120BPM because that's the solution that fits within the assumed ranges.

▶ SLp-2 requires that Reaktor's Master Clock be running in order to play. If you hear nothing, try clicking the play button in the Ensemble Tool Bar.

Having arrived at a number of beats, the Beat Loop Module slices the sample into that number of pieces and "sequences" them in sync with MIDI clock or Reaktor's Master Clock, if no MIDI clock signal is provided. That allows you to shift the pitch (i.e. playback rate) of the individual slices without changing the rhythm.

Instrument Structure
of SLp-2 with inset
showing the Macro
Structure for quantiz-
ing the start and loop
parameters to ¹⁄₁₆-
notes.

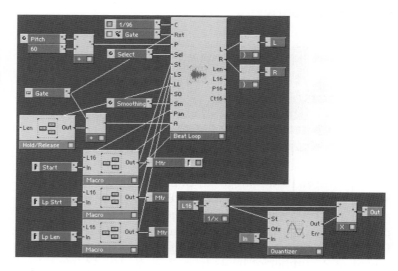

Like the Control Panel, the Structure of SLp-2 is almost identical to SLp-1. The differences are:

◆   Pitch is now separate from sample selection. The *Pitch*
    knob adjusts the pitches of the individual slices rather
    than the loop speed.

◆   The *Smoothing* knob smooths out the transition between
    individual slices by providing crossfade envelopes be-
    tween them.

◆   The *Start*, *Lp Start* and *Lp Len* sliders are now calibrated
    in slices using the quantizing Macro shown in the inset.
    That uses the length of the sample in ¹⁄₁₆-notes as re-
    ported at the Beat Loop Module's *L16* output to set the
    quantize step size.

SLp-3: Sample Lookup

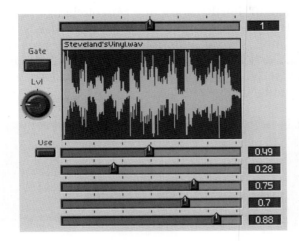

Instrument Control Panel for the Sample Lookup Ensemble. Playback of the sample proceeds forward and backward to the breakpoints indicated by the horizontal sliders at the bottom.

The SLp-3 Ensemble uses Reaktor's Sample Lookup Module to play a zig-zag path through a sample. The horizontal sliders set the breakpoints in the path—each time playback hits a slider's pointer position, it continues by playing to the next slider's position. Playback starts at the beginning of the sample when the *Gate* button is pressed or a MIDI Gate is received, except when the *Use* button is off, playback starts at the position indicated by the top slider. (That enables you to start playback in the middle of the sample.)

⊚ **45** SLp-3

Unlike Reaktor's other sampler Modules, Sample Lookup holds one sample at a time and that is loaded using Sample Lookup's context menu (right-click on the Module) rather than its Properties window. The Module has inputs for playback amplitude (*A*) and position within the sample in milliseconds (*Pos*). There are outputs for the values of the left and right channels of the sample at the position indicated, as well as an output for the total sample length in milliseconds.

In order to play back a sample at its normal speed in the Sample Lookup Module, you need to change the value at the

Pos input from zero (beginning of sample) to the sample length (end of sample) in an amount of time equal to the sample length. Furthermore, the rate-of-change needs to be constant (i. e. the sample playback path needs to be a straight line). Any variation from those constraints will alter the speed and direction of playback. That is, of course, exactly what we want—otherwise we'd just use a sample player and be done with it.

Instrument Structure of the SLp-3 sample lookup player.

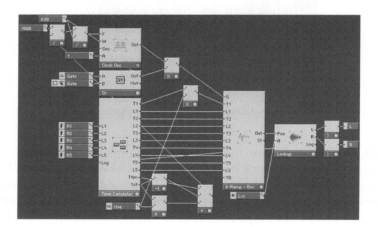

In SLp-3 the position of the Sample Lookup Module is controlled by a 6-Ramp Env Module, which generates six linear ramps with independent control of time and level for each ramp. The heart of SLp-3 is the Time Calculator Macro used to calculate the time and level for each ramp segment. It also calculates the total time for all ramps and uses that to control the frequency of the Clock Osc Module that gates the 6-Ramp Env Module. The time of the first ramp (*1st* output) is subtracted from the total time, then added back in if the *Use* button is on. Also, the *T1* output of the Time Calculator is only passed to the *T1* input of the 6-Ramp Env Module if the button is on. (I. e. when the *Use* button is off, the first ramp time is subtracted from the total time and first ramp time is set to zero, so that playback snaps instantly to the first breakpoint.)

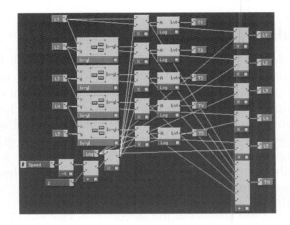

Macro Structure for the Time Calculator.

The Time Calculator Macro looks more complicated than it is because the same calculation is repeated for each ramp. Here are the details:

◆ The incoming slider values—which are between zero and one to indicate the position relative to the whole sample length—are multiplied by the total length of the sample in milliseconds. That gives the length in milliseconds from the beginning of the sample to the slider position.

◆ The segment length is used directly for the 6-Ramp Env Module's position inputs *L1* through *L5*.

◆ The |*x-y*| Macros calculate the absolute difference (i. e. larger value minus smaller value) between a slider and the one above it. That is the actual length of the segment to be played from one slider's position to the next's. (No |*x-y*| Macro is needed for the top slider.)

◆ The time calculation is converted to the dB/ms scale that the 6-Ramp Env Module's time inputs want to see. (See "Units and Conversions" on page 208.)

◆ All the extra Event Mult Modules are there to scale the times and levels with the *Speed* knob.

Granular Synthesis

Reaktor has three sampler Modules—ReSynth, Pitch Former and Grain Cloud—that use granular techniques to manipulate samples. ReSynth provides independent control of pitch and grain-sequence speed. Pitch Former alters the formants of the sound and offers independent pitch control as well. Grain Cloud provides the most extensive tools for grain sequencing. In our first sampler, we'll compare how ReSynth and Pitch Former can manipulate the same samples. Then we'll examine all of Grain Cloud's control options.

▶ You'll find the samplers in this section—GS-1, GS-2 and GS-3—in the Samplers folder inside the Ensembles folder on the WIZOO CD.

GS-1: Resynth and Pitch Former

Control Panel of GS-1 for comparing the effects of the Sampler ReSynth and Pitch Former Modules

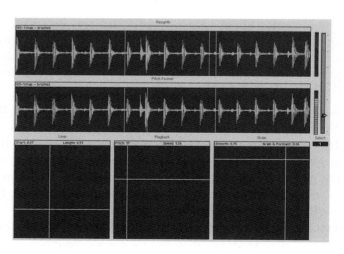

GS-1 illustrates the Sampler Resynth and Pitch Former Modules. The same sample Map is loaded into both Modules. It contains a groove-loop, a drum-loop, sung and spoken vocals and a waveset. Each of these can be processed in different ways in both Resynth and Pitch Former. Try out the Snapshots and play with the XY controls to get a feeling for what they can do.

46 Sampler Resynth

The leftmost XY Module sets the playback-loop start-point and length. It is calibrated in $1/128$'s of the total sample length, which makes it possible to hit the correct loop points in most wavesets and even-meter sample-loops. The middle XY Module controls the resynthesis pitch and grain-sequencing speed (more on that later). The right-most XY Module controls grain-smoothing and either grain size (Resynth) or formant shift (Pitch Former). The vertical slider is a bipolar control (see "BiPolar Knob" on page 206)—the lower half controls the level of the Pitch Former output and the upper half the Resynth output. (Both Resynth and Pitch Former are looping all the time, but only one is audible at a time.)

47 Pitch Former

The Sampler Resynth Module breaks the sample into short segments called grains, typically between 10 and 100 milliseconds in duration. The speed with which it plays an individual grain determines the pitch of that grain and is calibrated to the sample's Root Key (as specified in Resynth's Properties). That means if you match Resynth's pitch (P) input with the sample's Root Key, the grains will play at their natural rate. The rate at which the individual grains are sent out (which we'll call the grain-sequencing speed) is completely independent of the grain's playback speed and that is what determines the playback tempo. (That might be easier to visualize if you imagine the grains being individual beats of a beat-loop sample.) By adjusting the grain size and smoothing or crossfading between grains (use the right XY Module), you can alter the pitch and tempo of playback independently within a reasonable range. Pushing the effect to extremes can be interesting too.

▶ A pitch setting equal to the sample's specified Root Key and a speed setting of one, will play the looped part of the sample at its natural pitch and tempo regardless of the grain size. You'll only notice the effect of grain size and smoothing when you move away from the natural settings.

▶ For another look at Resynth, try out the factory Plasma Ensemble, which is also provided in the Factory folder inside the Ensembles folder on the WIZOO CD.

Pitch Former uses a different, but similar process. It uses the formant (i. e. FFT) information in small chunks of the sample to shift the chunks pitch and formant structure independently. (You can think of formants simply as resonances in the harmonic structure of the sound.) That process is not really granular, but it has similar properties. One thing that differentiates Pitch Former from Resynth is that Pitch Former does not rely on the Root Key setting of the sample (in fact, there is no Root Key setting in Pitch Former's Properties). Instead, it uses the formant analysis to resynthesize the sound, trying to achieve the pitch specified at its P input. In the process, it can also shift the formant structure. Pitch Former is especially useful with vocal samples, but it can be effective in many contexts. Use the center xy Module for pitch and the right-most xy Module for formant shifting. As with Resynth, "grain-sequencing" speed is independent of pitch (and also of formant shift).

▶ A pitch setting of zero, speed setting of one and formant shift of 0.5 will always play the looped part of the sample at its natural pitch and tempo. Pitch shifting is most effective with un-pitched samples. Formant shifting is always effective, but will produce considerable pitch shifting when you start with pitched sounds.

▶ For another look at Pitch Former try out the factory Diktaphon Ensemble, which is also provided in the Factory folder inside the Ensembles folder on the WIZOO CD.

GS-2: Grain Cloud

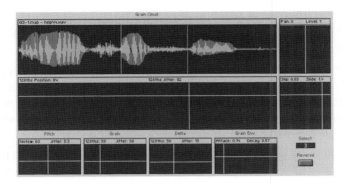

Control Panel for the
GS-2 Grain Cloud
sampler.

The Grain Cloud Module is the newest and most sophisticated of Reaktor's granular samplers. It allows you to manipulate and randomize (referred to as "Jitter") every aspect of
grain playback. The GS-2 Ensemble gives you access to each
input parameter using XY Modules. In most cases the horizontal direction controls some parameter value and the vertical direction controls the amount of Jitter. For a sophisticated example from the factory library of a sequencing-sam-
pler based on Grain Cloud see "GrainStates" on page 63.

The top window of the GS-2 Ensemble Control Panel shows
the selected sample from Grain Cloud's sample Map. This is
the same Map we used in GS-1 (see "GS-1: Resynth and Pitch
Former" on page 158). The large window below the sample
display is an XY control for selecting the grain position within
the sample. In GS-2, the only way to get any grain position
motion is using Jitter (in GS-3 we'll get more active). Both position and jitter are calibrated in $\frac{1}{128}$'s of the total sample
length, which is convenient for beat-loops and wavesets. The
XY controls to the right of the sample display controls volume
(vertical) and pan position (horizontal). The XY control below
that controls pan Jitter and pitch-slide (see below). The four
XY controls along the bottom respectively control pitch, grain

◎ **48** GS-2

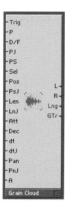

size, time between grains and the grain AD envelope. Horizontal position sets the parameter value and vertical position sets the amount of Jitter.

Here are the ins and outs of Grain Cloud, divided into several basic categories:

◆ Pitch is controlled by three inputs: *P*, *PJ* and *PS*. *P* sets the pitch of grain playback calibrated in MIDI note numbers. *PJ* sets the amount of Jitter (randomness) in semitones around the current pitch. *PS* sets the amount pitch-slide that occurs during the playback of each grain.

◆ There are five grain parameters: *D/F*, *Len*, *Lnj*, *Att* and *Dec*. *D/F* controls whether the grain plays forward (value ≥0) or backward (value <0). *Len* and *Lnj* set the grain size and Jitter range in milliseconds. (It is often convenient to set this as a proportion of the total sample length as we do in GS-2.) *Att* and *Dec* set the attack and decay times of the grain envelope in dB/ms (see "Units and Conversions" on page 208).

◆ Three parameters control where the grain comes from: *Sel*, *Pos* and *Psj*. *Sel* selects the sample in Grain Cloud's sample Map. *Pos* selects the position within the sample in milliseconds and, like *Len*, it is often convenient to use fractions of the total sample length. *Lnj* controls the amount of position Jitter in milliseconds.

◆ Output level and stereo pan position are controlled by the *A*, *Pan* and *Pnj* inputs. As you might guess, *Pnj* controls the pan Jitter.

◆ Grain sequencing is controlled using the *Trig*, *dt* and *dtj* inputs. A positive event at *Trig* will immediately trigger the next grain. (Note that any change at the *Sel* input does not take effect until a grain change. If you want immediate selection, accompany selection changes with triggers.) *dt* and *dtj* set the time to the next grain and time-Jitter, respectively. Grain Cloud is always playing—there is no

Loop or Loop in Release Properties that need to be turned on as with the other sampler Modules.

◆ The *Lng* output reports the length of the selected sample in milliseconds. That is handy when you want to set some parameters (e. g. *Len*, *dt*, *Pos*, etc.) as a fraction of the sample length.

◆ The *GTrg* output sends a trigger each time a new grain is triggered. That is useful, for example, for triggering envelope generators when using long grains.

▶ Keep in mind when using Grain Cloud that there are two fundamental ways to use grains: for sequencing large chunks of a sample (like beats of a beat-loop) and for creating complex sounds by rapidly sequencing very short grains (e. g. from a waveset). In the first case, *Len* and *dt* are generally large (i. e. hundreds of milliseconds) and in the latter, they are small (i. e. between 1 and 100ms).

GS-3: Moving Grains

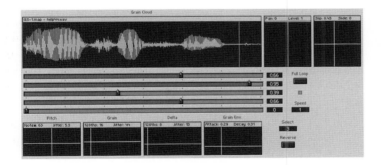

Ensemble Control Panel for GS-3, adding motion automation to GS-2.

One way to enliven Grain Cloud is to add some motion to the grain position. We do this in GS-3 using a 6-Ramp Env Module in a way similar to what we did with the Sample Lookup Module. (See "SLp-3: Sample Lookup" on page 155.)

⊚ **49** GS-3

The five horizontal sliders set position targets. Times to reach those targets are calculated relative to the total sample length and sequenced using the ramps of the 6-Ramp envelope. When the *Full Loop* button is turned on, the loop will start and end at the beginning of the sample. When it is turned off, the loop starts at the stop slider position and ends at the bottom slider position. The LED flashes to indicate each envelope cycle. The rest of the GS-3 controls are the same as in GS-2.

5 Building a Sequencer

In this section we'll examine several approaches to building step-sequencers in Reaktor. We'll start out with clocks since every step-sequencer needs a propeller. Next, we'll use two forms of step-sequencer Modules to build a pitch-and-velocity sequencer with a couple of unusual twists. Then, we'll use Event Table Modules to build an asynchronous pitch-and-velocity sequencer in much the same way we used the Audio Table to build a wavetable synthesizer (see WT-1: Wavetable Synthesis" on page 128).

▶ You'll find the clock and sequencers in this section—Clocks, Sqx-1 and Sqx-2—in the Sequencers folder inside the Ensembles folder on the WIZOO CD.

Clocks: Pulse-Clocks and MIDI Sync

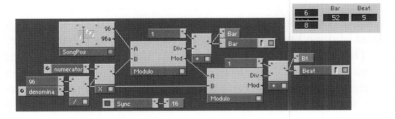

Macro Structure and Control Panel for a metronome/clock which can be used to clock a step-sequencer or an audible metronome.

In Reaktor, you can clock a step-sequencer in two ways: using Reaktor's Master Clock (which can be synchronized to MIDI Clock) or using some kind of oscillator to generate clock pulses. We'll start with Reaktor's Master Clock.

The Metro Macro shown here derives its timing from the SongPos Module, which sends a new event every 1/96-note when Reaktor's Master Clock is running. The value at the 96 and *96a* outputs is the number of ¹⁄₉₆-notes since the last Master Clock reset. (You reset the Master Clock by double-clicking the Stop button of the Master Clock in the Ensemble Toolbar; see "Reaktor's Toolbars" on page 16).

▶ ¹⁄₉₆-note means ¹⁄₉₆ of a whole-note, which is the same as ¹⁄₂₄ of a quarter-note. In other words, Reaktor's Master Clock runs at 24 pulses-per-quarter (ppq).

The Metro Macro has controls on the left for setting a time signature and displays on the right for the bar and beat count as communicated by the SongPos Module. That involves first calculating how many ¹⁄₉₆-notes are in a bar and in a beat. The number of ¹⁄₉₆-notes in a beat is calculated by dividing the bottom number in the time-signature into 96. Multiplying that result by the number of beats in a bar (the top number in the time-signature) gives the number of ¹⁄₉₆-notes in a bar.

To set the *Bar* display, we divide the ¹⁄₉₆-note count (the output of the SongPos Module) by the number of ¹⁄₉₆-notes in a bar. We use the Modulo Module for that—its *Div* output is the whole-number part of the division and its *Mod* output is the remainder (i. e. the number of ¹⁄₉₆-notes into the next bar). Divide the remainder by the number of ¹⁄₉₆-notes in a beat and we know how many beats into the next bar we are.

The Metro Macro has outputs for the bar count, the beat count and for a ¹⁄₁₆-note pulse. The pulse is generated by the Sync Module, whose Properties can be set to make it generate any of the common note increments. By changing the Sync Module's Properties, you can directly create any pulse you want. You can also use Modulo Modules at the *Bar* and *Bt* outputs to generate pulses at any number of bars and beats. That makes Metro a very flexible tempo-based clock. Have a look at the MetroSnd Module in the Ensemble, where that technique is used to generate audible bars-and-beats clicks.

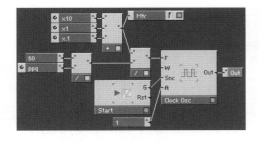

Another—and more straightforward—way to build a clock is with a pulse oscillator. Reaktor's Clock Osc Module is designed to do that in the most CPU-efficient way. It generates variable-width pulse events that can be synchronized to any desired start signal. In the example we've used a Start Module for that. The Start Module generates a gate at its *G* output whenever Reaktor's Master Clock is started. (That doesn't sync the Clock Osc to Reaktor's clock, but it does restart it in sync.)

The only trick in the PPQ Clock Macro is setting the oscillator frequency. First we add up the values of the three knobs (used to set tempo in 2-digit precision), then divide that sum by the desired number of clock-pulses per beat (i. e. by 60/*PPB*).

The little slider below the *PPB* numerical sets the pulse-width. It can be used to control note duration when the PPQ Clock is used to generate gates.

Sqx-1: Basic Step Sequencer

Instrument Control Panel for the Sqx-1 step-sequencer. The sliders are for pitch and the knobs for velocity. The LEDs indicate the active pitch and velocity step, which can be rotated to any desired relationship.

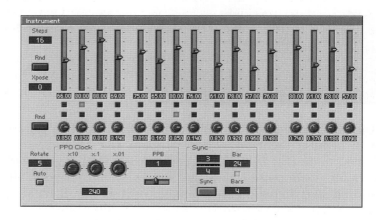

50   Sqx-1

Sqx-1 uses two of Reaktor's step-sequencing Modules: 16-Step and Select 16. Both are 16-step sequencers, but while the 16-Step Module increments one step each time it receives a clock pulse, the Select 16 Module has a position (*Pos*) input for selecting its position. We've used 16-Step for the pitch sequence and Select 16 for the velocity-gates. 16-Step has an output (*Stp*) that tells its current step and that, with an offset added, is used to select the Select 16 step. The *Rotate* numerical sets the offset and a Modulo Module is used to ensure that the Select 16 position "rolls over" regardless of the sequence length. (For example, for a four step sequence, an offset of six will be the same as an offset of two.) The two rows of LEDs indicate the current position in the pitch and gate-velocity sequences.

▶ In the Sqx-1 Ensemble, the sequencer is hooked up to play a two-operator FM synth (see "FM-1: Two-Operator FM Synth" on page 120).

Other features of Sqx-1 include randomize (*Rnd*) buttons for the pitch sliders and velocity knobs, a selector for the number of steps in the sequence and an auto-rotate button, which increases the *Rotate* setting each time the pitch sequence loops to step 1. Because of the use of two clocks (see below), that can produce very complex pitch-accent patterns. (For a look at how the *Rnd* buttons work, see "Control Randomizer" on page 200.)

The main clock for Sqx-1 is the PPQ Clock described earlier (see "Clocks: Pulse-Clocks and MIDI Sync" on page 165). That clock always determines the sequence speed. The Sync clock to its right is a modified version of the Metro clock and is used to generate a sequencer reset every so many bars at the indicated time-signature. It is only active when the *Sync* button is on and Reaktor's Master Clock is running. With Reaktor's Master Clock running at a different tempo than the Sqx-1 clock, you will get a repeating reset pattern that is out of sync with Sqx-1's natural looping. With auto-rotation also turned on, you'll get a much more complex pitch-accent pattern than a simple 16-step step-sequencer can generate on its own.

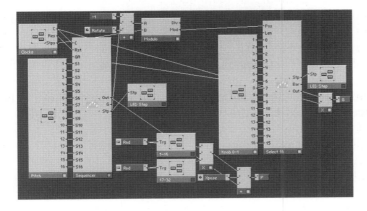

Here's the layout of the Sqx-1 structure:

◆ The Pitch and Knob Macros contain the banks of 16 knobs and sliders. They are cosmetically modified from similar Macros in the factory library. The only reason for encapsulating the controls is to simplify the layout.

◆ The 1—16 and 17—32 Macros are used to randomize the controls (see "Control Randomizer" on page 200).

◆ The clocking and synchronization circuitry is in the Clocks Macro (see "Clocks: Pulse-Clocks and MIDI Sync" on page 165).

◆ The LEDs are lit by the LED Step Macros shown here. Each Lamp Module has its range set so that it lights for indicated step number and is dark otherwise. (The Event Merge Module prevents flickering.)

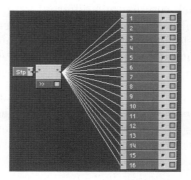

You'll find the Sqx-1 sequencer Instrument by itself in the Instruments folder on the WIZOO CD.

Sqx-2: Event Table Sequencer

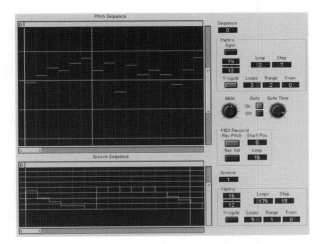

Instrument Control Panel for Sqx-2, an asynchronous pitch-and-gate step sequencer with MIDI recording.

Whereas Sqx-1 emulates traditional step-sequencers—with a small number of steps and with knobs and sliders for setting the step values—Sqx-2 is a modern-day version featuring 16,384 steps and graphic or MIDI data entry. Like Sqx-1, there are separate sequencers for pitch and velocity, but in Sqx-2 they run on completely independent clocks. (I. e. the pitch and velocities are asynchronous.)

⊚ **51** Sqx-2

Sqx-2 uses Event Table Modules for its pitch and velocity sequences. Each table is 128-by-128 and you can use it as one long sequence (up to 16,384 steps) or as 128 128-note sequences. The *Y-cycle* buttons in the Metro sections switch between modes.

Here are some things to keep in mind about using the Event Tables:

◆ The vertical and horizontal scroll-bars control both the viewing position and the zoom of the table display. Click on the right end, where the arrow is, to change the zoom.

- There are light vertical gridlines for each sequence step and bold gridlines every 16 steps.
- The horizontal gridlines in the pitch sequence are at octaves, while those in the groove sequence are in steps of 16.
- You can enter and change values in the tables by clicking or click-dragging with the mouse.
- You can manipulate multiple events by using the Event Table's context-menu (right-click in the display). There are interesting options once you've selected some events, such as mirroring, scaling and rotating the selection.

The Sqx-2 Ensemble Structure is fairly simple. Two modified metronome-clocks (see "Clocks: Pulse-Clocks and MIDI Sync" on page 165) control the read-positions in the Event Tables that contain the pitch and velocity sequences. The MIDI Record Macro controls the write positions and routes incoming MIDI data accordingly. A Slew Limiter Module is used for adding glide (a. k. a. portamento or glissando) to the pitch sequence and a Hold Module that can be switched in and out is used to provide optional variable-width gates. (When switched out, notes are gated for the full width of the step and in both cases new gates are generated only when the velocity changes.)

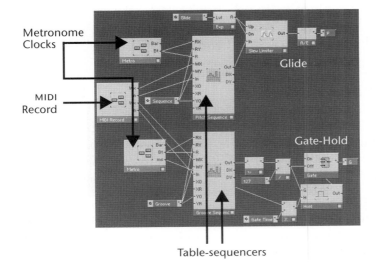

Metronome
Clocks

MIDI
Record

Glide

Gate-Hold

Sqx-2 Ensemble
Structure.

Table-sequencers

Reaktor's Event Table Modules work almost exactly like the Audio Table Modules we used in our wavetable synths (see WT-1: Wavetable Synthesis" on page 128). In this case, they are set up to have 128 columns and 128 rows with the row number (0 to 127) being the sequence number and the column (i. e. position) number being the step number in the sequence. In other words, the Module's *RY* input selects one of the 128 sequences and the *RX* input is used to step through the sequence.

▶ Unlike the Audio Table, which produces an output each time the RX or RY input changes, the Event Table's output needs to be triggered. The R input is for that.

The sequence-playback timing is controlled by the metronome-clock we saw earlier (see "Clocks: Pulse-Clocks and MIDI Sync" on page 165), which means that it is synchronized to Reaktor's Master Clock. Although the time-signature numericals (top- and bottom-left) work exactly the same way, they have a little different meaning here.

Metronome-clock
Control Panel (top)
and circuitry for con-
trolling Y-cycling
(bottom).

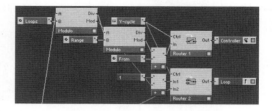

The bottom time-signature numerical sets step size and the top one sets the sequence length in steps. The step size is represented as divisions of a whole note (e. g. 12 for a ¹⁄₁₂-note, meaning ¹⁄₈-note triplets). The *Loop* display shows the number of loops since the last Master Clock reset or since the last change of sequence if the *Y-cycle* button is turned on. The *Step* display shows the current sequence step.

The *Y-cycle* button controls whether a single sequence (i. e. row of the Event Table) plays or whether Sqx-2 cycles through several sequences. In the latter case, the *Loops* numerical determines the loop count at which the sequence changes, the *Range* numerical determines how many sequences are used and the *From* numerical determines the first of the sequences (i. e. *RY* values).

The Y-cycle circuitry is shown at the bottom of the illustration. The Modulo Modules divide the loop-count by the *Loops* setting then takes the remainder of division by the *Range* setting. That just gives the current Y-cycle step. The *From* setting is added to that to get the correct *RY* value, which is then routed to a MIDI Controller Output Module for remotely setting the *Sequence* numerical. (The Modules in red are used to change the *Loop* display from absolute to relative counting.)

▶ The important thing to remember is that there are completely independent metronome-clocks for the pitch and velocity (labeled
"Groove") sequencers. That means, for example, that you could have
short and simple groove sequence controlling the gating and accents
of a long and complex pitch sequence.

▶ When the *Sync* button in the top metronome-clock is turned on, time-
signature settings made there will also change the bottom metronome-clock.

The *Gate* and *Gate-Time* controls may seem a little obscure
at first. When gating is turned off, a new event appears at
Sqx-2's *G* output every time the velocity value changes. Depending on the synth or sampler being played by Sqx-2, this
will most likely re-trigger some envelopes and possibly affect
the envelope amounts. But there will only be a release phase
when the next step has value zero (i. e. no gate). When gating
is turned on, a Hold Module is used to send out a pulse,
whose width is controlled by the *Gate* setting scaled to the
step-duration. In that case, the hold and release phases will
be determined by the pulse width.

MIDI Record Control
Panel and Structure.

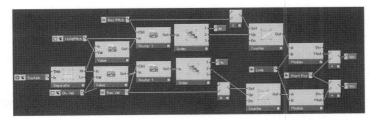

The MIDI Record Macro controls the X write-position *WX* of
the Event Table Modules. When recording is enabled for the
pitch sequencer, incoming MIDI Note-ons first have their

note-number written to the current position in the table, then are used to increment a counter that rolls over after the number of steps indicated in the *Loop* numerical. Whenever recording is turned on (*Rec Pitch* button), the counter and *WX* are reset to the value in the *Start Pos* numerical. The only difference for velocity recording is that the Note-on velocity is recorded rather than the note-number. In both cases, the MIDI Sustain Pedal (Controller 64) is set up to write the previous value to the current position and increment the counter. When velocity is being recorded, that ensures that new gates aren't generated—i. e. it results in a legato effect.

As with Sqx-1, the Ensemble comes with a two-operator FM synth and the sequencer Instrument is also available in the Instruments folder on the WIZOO CD.

6 Filters and Other Effects

Building effects processors in Reaktor is a big enough topic for a book of its own. You can get some idea of the wide range of possibilities in the GeekFX factory Ensemble (see "GeekFX" on page 75). You'll also find effects built in to many of the factory Ensembles—particularly distortion, delay/echo and reverberation effects.

We'll spend most of the time in this section building and analyzing effects made with two closely related Module types: filters and delay lines. We'll also investigate one kind of distortion technique—waveshaping. Modulation techniques like FM, AM and ring modulation have been covered in the synthesizer and sampler sections, but keep in mind that they can also be applied as effects to any audio signal.

Monophonic versus polyphonic processing (see "Voices, Channels and Outputs" on page 21) is an important consideration when building effects. Effects tend to be CPU-intensive and using them polyphonically, obviously, multiplies the problem. Unless some aspect of the effect is controlled by individual-voice information (e. g. delay time via MIDI Note-on Velocity), there is probably no advantage in polyphonic processing. If you make an effect into its own Instrument, individual voice information is lost anyway, so you might as well make it a one-voice Instrument. In cases where you do need polyphonic effect processing, build the effect into the polyphonic Instrument generating the sound it is processing.

▶ Remember not to make it an Instrument within the Instrument—make it a Macro instead.

The first three effects in this section are mainly for illustration. Each contains three related processes and four oscilloscopes—one for the input signal and three to show the ef-

fects of the processing. There's also a central knob for selecting which signal to hear. Don't worry that this is a complete
waste of time—we'll apply some of these processes in more
useful effects later in the chapter.

FTC: The UnFilters

▶ You'll find the FTC Ensemble in the Effects folder inside the Ensembles
folder on the WIZOO CD.

The FTC Ensemble dis-
plays the results of
differentiation and
integration of asym-
metric triangle and
parabolic waveforms
as well as an additive
harmonics waveset.

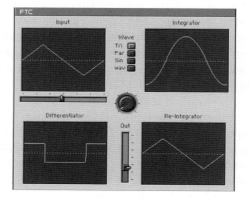

The Differentiator and Integrator Modules are two of Reaktor's more unusual filters. The Differentiator calculates the
rate-of-change of the samples of the incoming signal. The Integrator adds the incoming sample values. The remarkable
thing here is that if you follow either of these processes by
the other, you will get the original signal back—except for
any DC-offset. (In math circles, that is known as the Fundamental Theorem of Calculus.)

▶ A signal with a DC offset will drive the Integrator nuts (i.e. the sum
will keep growing over time). For that reason, it's a good idea to pre-
cede the Integrator with a highpass filter whose cutoff frequency is

zero. That will remove the DC offset without seriously affecting the incoming signal.

The Differentiator measures the rate at which the incoming values are changing and reports that value at its output. A triangle-wave provides a good illustration: the sides of the triangle, being straight lines, represent a constant rate of change. Therefore, the Differentiator's output is a positive constant value during the up-sloping sides of the triangle and an equivalent, negative constant during the down-sloping sides. What better way to describe a square wave?

Beneath the *Input* oscilloscope display is a slider for controlling the symmetry of the triangle wave. Move it and you'll notice that one side of the triangle gets shorter and steeper while the other side gets longer and shallower. Look at the *Differentiator* oscilloscope and you'll notice the pulse-width changing and the waveform becoming offset vertically. (The offset results from the difference in the slopes of the sides.)

Use the *Wave* button to try the parabolic (*Par*) and sine (*Sin*) waveforms. (The symmetry slider affects the parabolic, but not the sine waveform.) You'll see that a parabolic wave differentiates into a triangle, but that a sine wave differentiates into a sine wave with a 90-degree phase offset.

Finally, look at the other oscilloscopes. The one at the bottom-right shows the result of applying the Integrator after the Differentiator and you'll see that it always reproduces the original waveform. The oscilloscope on the top-right shows the result of applying the Integrator to the original waveform.

The pictures and math are all well and good, but the important thing is what's happening to the sound. The four-position knob in the center allows you to listen to the signal shown in the oscilloscope to which it is pointing.

▶ If you start Reaktor's MIDI transport, it will automatically cycle through the four outputs in half-note steps at the current tempo. If you're curious how that's done, see "Automated Knob" on page 205.

In more conventional terms, you can think of the Differentiator as a kind of lowpass un-filter—it gives a frequency-dependent boost to frequencies above 159Hz. The Integrator does just the opposite, which you can think of as highpass un-filtering. It gives a frequency-dependent boost to frequencies below 159Hz. For example, you can create a triangle wave by passing a square wave through a lowpass filter and, as we've seen and heard, the Differentiator does the opposite, turning a triangle wave into a square wave.

▶ Select the wav input using the *Wave* buttons and play with the symmetry slider to hear the effects of these filters on more complex waveforms.

The Shape of Things

▶ You'll find the Shapers Ensemble in the Effects folder inside the Ensembles folder on the WIZOO CD.

Ensemble Control Panel for three forms of waveshaping: breakpoint, multiplication and wavetable.

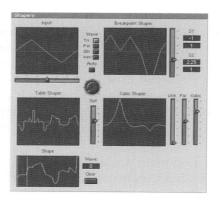

53 Shapers

Waveshaping is often lumped in with the modulation techniques discussed in Chapter 3 "Building a Synthesizer". Like FM, it can be used to create a rich harmonic spectrum in a computationally simple fashion. Reaktor provides two categories of audio waveshaping Modules—breakpoint shapers and multiplying shapers—and it is also a simple matter to construct your own waveshaping patterns using the Audio Table Module. The Shapers Ensemble shown here illustrates all three methods.

Waveshaping uses some amplitude-mapping process to change the shape of a waveform. Breakpoint waveshaping multiplies all values above or below a threshold value, called the breakpoint, by some factor. Compression is a familiar example of that process. Parabolic and cubic waveshaping multiple the incoming values by themselves two or three times, respectively. Waveshaping by an Audio Table replaces the incoming values—interpreted as the cell number—by the value in the cell. If you think of the row of cells as a waveform (see "WT-1: Wavetable Synthesis" on page 128), you'll have the idea of one waveform shaping another.

Shapers

The Shapers Ensemble is similar to the FTC Ensemble (see page 178). The top-left scope shows in the original waveform while the other three scopes show the results of the three kinds of waveshaping. The same source waveforms are provided except that the samples now are loops (use the horizontal slider to select the loop). The audio output is selected by the knob in the middle (which is not automated this time). The relevant controls for breakpoint and cubic shaping are to the right of their respective scopes and the Audio Table display and wave selector are below the *Table Shaper* scope.

Waveshaping

Waveshaping can be used as a static or dynamic process. As a static process, it changes the shape of a waveform. If the amplitude of the waveform is also changing (for example, being controlled by an envelope) then the effect of waveshaping changes over time—i. e. is dynamic. The *Auto* button turns on a clock-triggered Hold-Release envelope generator with about a half-second release time to illustrate the dynamic effect. The beat loops also illustrate dynamic waveshaping.

Breakpoint Shaper

For the Breakpoint Shaper, the slider sets both the positive and negative thresholds. (The thresholds can also be controlled separately.) The top numerical of each pair sets the slope by which the values above and below the thresholds are scaled. Start with a triangle or sine wave and play with the numericals (with the slider near the middle of its range) and you'll immediately get the picture. Values between zero and one are like compression and values above one are like expansion. The other two numericals shape the part of the waveform between the thresholds.

Cubic Shaper

The Cubic Shaper mixes the unaltered input with squared (*Par* slider) and cubed (*Cubic* slider) outputs. As opposed to breakpoint shaping, which typically produces in-harmonic distortion, this shaper tends to produce a lot of harmonics. When applied dynamically, it's great for generating plucked sounds.

Table Shaper

The Table Shaper remaps the incoming signal using the selected wavetable. Needless to say, you can draw in your own waves and the results are as varied as your dexterity with the mouse. The Audio Table Module is set up to hold 32 waveforms. Try Snapshots 1, 4, 5, 6 and 9 for a variety of effects and keep in mind that the left half of the table shapes the negative part of the incoming signal while the right half shapes the positive part.

Phase Cancellation with Short Delays

▶ You'll find the Delays Ensemble in the Effects folder inside the Ensembles folder on the WIZOO CD.

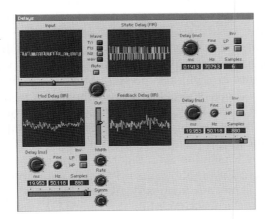

The Delays Ensemble illustrates the relation between short delays and filtering via phase cancellation. Top-right mixes equal parts of the delayed and original signal. Bottom-right adds feedback. Bottom-left adds an LFO for delay time to produce flanging and phasing.

◎ **54** Delays

Delay lines with short delay times (generally under 50ms) can be used to produce a wide variety of filtering effects. In fact, in the time domain, digital filters are constructed by mixing the outputs of multiple delay lines and using other delay lines to feed the signal back to the input. A general discussion of filter design is beyond the scope of both this book and its author, but a simple example will give you the basic idea.

If you delay a sine wave by half a cycle and mix it back with itself, the two signals will cancel. It's a little less obvious, but true, that any amount of delay will result in a sine wave whose amplitude is between zero and twice the original. Since the cycle time—which in milliseconds, is 1,000 divided by the frequency—gets shorter as the frequency gets higher, shorter delay times correspond to the cancellation of higher frequencies.

If you think of a complex waveform as a mix of sine waves, then mixing a delayed copy with itself will reinforce some of the sine wave components and partially cancel others. The main point here is that no new frequencies are added; only the amplitudes of the existing component frequencies are changed. For very short delay times (on the order of a few samples) the result is a form of lowpass filtering. Inverting either signal (the original or the delayed) reverses the cancellation/reinforcement pattern and, therefore, for very short delays, results in highpass filtering. Various modifications— longer delay times (still below 50ms), the use of feedback, the use of more delay lines, modifying the amounts of the various components in the mix, modulating the delay times, etc.—produce more complex kinds of filtering. The purpose of the Delays Ensemble is to illustrate some of these effects.

The Delays Ensemble Control Panel is undoubtedly familiar by now. The four scopes display the original signal and three kinds of processing while the round knob in the center selects the audio output. The *Wave* buttons select the source—in this case variable width triangle and pulse waves, a noise source and a loop player. The frequency of the waveforms is 100Hz and you should keep that in mind when analyzing the delay time settings. The *Auto* button starts a repeating decay envelope because, as with the waveshaping, short pulses illustrate the effects well.

All three effects incorporate a single delay line with coarse and fine tuning knobs for the delay time. The delay time is displayed in milliseconds, Hertz and samples (at 44,100Hz sampling rate) and the range is one sample to 100ms. The bottom two effects add feedback and produce what are known as infinite-impulse-response filters. (The non-feedback version at the top-right is called finite-impulse response.) The bottom-left effect adds a variable-shape LFO for delay time modulation. That produces flanging and phasing effects.

As with the Shapers and FTC Ensembles, the Delays Ensemble is meant to illustrate the effect of short time delays. A good approach is to listen to the Snapshots, then start tweaking the various controls. Finally, look at the Structures (discussed below) to get ideas about incorporating the Delay Line Modules in your own Ensembles. Here are some structural elements worth pointing out:

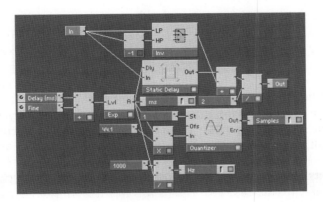

Macro Structure of the Static Delay (FIR).

- The delay-time controls are shaped by a Exp(A) Module so that the delay-time changes slowly at low values and more rapidly later. That makes it easier to dial in very short delay times. (See "Units and Conversions" on page 208.)

- Because the knob ranges are scaled to produce the desired values after shaping, their value displays are not useful. Meters with their graphic turned off have been used instead to display the delay in milliseconds, Hertz (which is calculated by dividing the delay time into 1,000) and samples at a 44,100 Hertz sampling rate.

- The *Inv* switch selects whether a normal or inverted version of the input is mixed into the output. The effect is to toggle between lowpass and highpass filtering at very short delay times, hence the switch labels.

Macro Structure of the Feedback Delay (IIR). The red Modules indicate the added feedback circuitry.

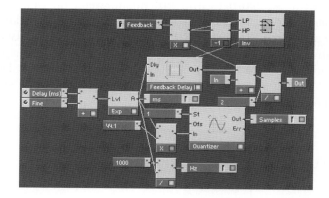

◆ When feedback is added the signal path changes. Here the input is mixed directly with the Feedback Delay Module's output and the mixed output is either inverted or not, then sent to the delay input.

Macro Structure of the Mod Delay (IIR). The red Modules indicate the added LFO modulation circuitry.

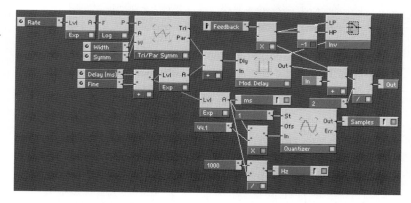

◆ The LFO adds the parabolic-wave output Tri/Par Symm Module to the static delay-time setting.

◆ The *Width* knob controls the LFO amplitude (i. e. the amount of variation above and below the delay-time setting).

- The *Symm* varies the parabolic shape from a curved, ramp-up through parabolic to a curved, ramp-down.
- The *Rate* control is first passed through an exponential shaper to make the early part of its range more sensitive than passed through logarithmic shaper to convert frequency to pitch as required by the oscillator's *P* input. (See "Units and Conversions" on page 208.)

Multi-tap Delay Lines

▶ You'll find the Taps and TapsVel Ensembles in the Effects folder inside the Ensembles folder on the WIZOO CD.

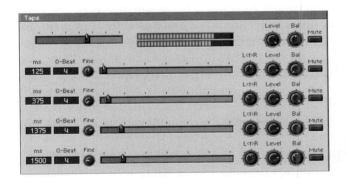

The Taps Ensemble includes a stereo, multi-tap delay (top) and a beat loop player (bottom) as a sound source.

Reaktor's Multi-Tap Delay Module makes constructing this stereo, four-tap, feedback delay Instrument almost a no-

◎ **55** Taps

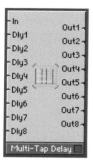

brainer. The Module supports up to eight taps and provides a separate output for each. In this Ensemble we've used two of the Modules, but only four taps on each. If you add any kind of sound source—as we've done with the Beat Looper Instrument (see "SLp-2: Beat Loops" on page 153)—four taps will already require a fast CPU. Beyond that, this effect can get pretty dense even with four taps. But, if you have a fast machine and want more taps, it will take you no time at all to copy the Tap Time Macros and wire them up to taps five through eight.

Before we get into the Structure, notice that the multi-tap effect, Taps, is implemented as an Instrument rather than as a Macro inside another Instrument. The reason is that it is, by its nature, a monophonic effect and putting it inside another Instrument will result in a lot of unnecessary CPU processing. The Taps Instrument is set to one voice, but it can be used to process the combined voices of a polyphonic Instrument. It can also be used with direct audio input. Later, we will modify it to let MIDI Note-on Velocity affect the tap levels and in that case, using it polyphonically makes sense. You'll find both Instrument and Macro forms of the Taps Instrument as well as a Macro of the velocity sensitive version on the WIZOO CD.

Each tap has coarse (horizontal) and fine (small knob) controls for setting the tap time. The range is zero to 10 seconds and the coarse adjustment is in 50ms steps while the fine adjustment is in 1ms steps. However, the *Q-Beat* numerical to the left of the *fine* knob can force the tap times to multiples of any beat division from a whole beat to a $1/16$'s of a beat (i. e. $1/64$-notes). For un-quantized control, set the *Q-Beat* numerical to zero. The tap times are displayed in the numericals at the far left.

The *Level* and *Bal* knobs set the level and balance in the stereo field for the input signal (top knobs) and each of the four taps. For the taps, the *L<f>R* knobs control the amount of feedback from the tap back to the left or right input. These

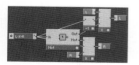

knobs are bi-polar: at the center, there is no feedback, moving the knob counterclockwise, increases the feedback to the left input and moving it clockwise increases the feedback to the right input. The circuitry for doing this (see illustration) is extremely simple (see "BiPolar Knob" on page 206).

The delay time setting as well as the input, output and feedback signal routing are controlled by the Tap Time Macros; there's one for each tap. The quantization amount (St) input of the Quantizer Module is set by dividing Reaktor's tempo into 1,000 (to get ms per beat) then dividing that by the value of the *Q-Beat* knob. The Tempo Info Module reports the tempo in beats-per-second, which is why 1,000 is used instead of 60,000 as would be done with BPM.

► When the Q-Beat knob is set to zero, Reaktor's X/Y Module kindly sends out zero rather than exploding in your face.

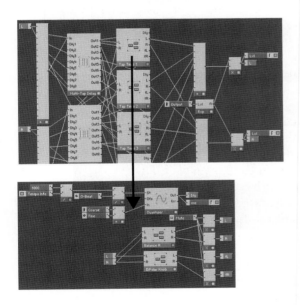

Most of the action in the Taps Instrument is in the Tap Time Macros (bottom), which control the tap times as well as the routing of the audio output and feedback.

The *L* and *R* inputs to the Tap Time Macro come from the tap outputs of the Multi-Tap Delay Modules. The signal passes through the Balance Macro, which controls both the volume and balance to the *L* and *R* outputs. It also passes through the BiPolar Knob Macro, which controls the level of the signal sent to the *fL* or *fR* outputs. These are wired back to the giant Audio Add Modules that mix the inputs to the Multi-Tap Delay Modules.

The TapsVel Ensemble inserts the four-tap delay as a Macro inside a polyphonic drum synth from the Reaktor factory library. It will, therefore, operate polyphonically (and take up more CPU).

The TapsVel Ensemble adds a polyphonic version of the four-tap delay to a basic percussion synth from the Reaktor factory library. The velocity with which you play the drum sounds controls the level of the multi-tap delay input for that voice.

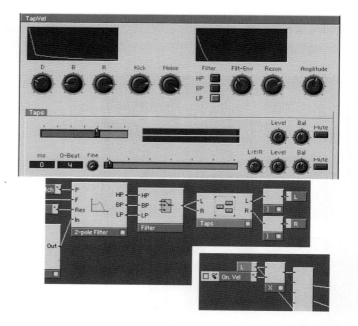

In order for polyphonic operation to make sense, individual voice information must have some effect on the tap processing. Here MIDI Note-on Velocity (via the On. Vel Module) is used to scale the input to the Multi-Tap Delay Modules. Therefore, loud notes will result in more input to the delays.

▶ Notice that the input to the Balance Macro that is used to control the direct signal is not scaled by velocity.

Reverberation

▶ You'll find the TwoVerbs Ensemble in the Effects folder inside the Ensembles folder on the WIZOO CD.

Control Panel and Ensemble Structure for monaural reverb unit. Two types of reverb are featured. The unit is placed between Reaktor's audio input and output Modules to process the playback of Reaktor's Audio File Player (bottom).

Realistic reverbs (i. e. emulating natural spaces) are among the most difficult effects to design as well as being among the most CPU-intensive. No attempt has been made for great realism here, but two typical styles of reverb circuits are illustrated. Both reverbs use Reaktor's Diffuser Delay Module, which is designed for this purpose. The Type I reverb (on the left) uses four Static Delay Modules in parallel followed by two Diffuser Delays in series. The Type II reverb (on the right) uses four Diffuser Delays in series with a highpass/

◎ **56** Type I Reverb

191

lowpass feedback delay loop. Both are standard reverb designs.

The Diffuser Delay Module is a feedback delay line, which as we've seen, with small delay times causes cancellation of some frequencies and reinforcement of others. With delay times in the 0.1 to 50ms range the effect is called a comb filter because the cancellation frequencies are spread out evenly over the spectrum in a pattern resembling the teeth of a comb. What makes the Diffuser Delay different than a simple comb filter is that some of the input signal is inverted and mixed in with the output. That reverses some of the cancellation/reinforcement effect (depending on the amount of signal mixed in) but leaves the frequency-dependent phase shift. When the comb effect is completely missing, the effect is called allpass filtering because no frequences are attenuated. With longer delay times, it produces a decaying series of echos.

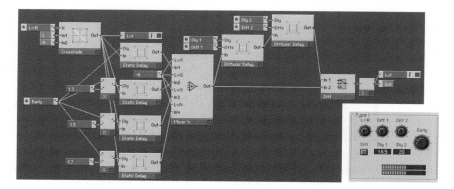

If you stack several Diffuser Delay Modules in series, you get a compounding of echos—i. e. echos of echos of echos—which is why these Modules are ideal for reverbs. Our Type I delay uses two Diffuser Delay Modules preceeded by four Static Delay Modules in parallel. Those function as a pre-delay circuit. For simplicity, the *Early* knob controls all the pre-delay times setting them in ratios of $1\times$, $1.3\times$, $1.5\times$ and $1.7\times$

the knob value. The *Diff 1* and *Diff 2* knobs control the amount feed-forward of the Diffuser Delay Modules (discussed above), which means the amount of comb filtering or "coloration". Fully counterclockwise, the result is pure delay (no feed-forward) and fully clockwise the Module is neutral— the input signal is passed through. The least coloration occurs with the knob in the middle of its range. The *Dly 1* and *Dly 2* numericals set the Diffuser Delay's delay times and the *Diff* button to their left takes the Diffuser Delays out of the circuit so you can audition and use the bank of Static Delays by themselves.

▶ You could just as well use a Multi-Tap Delay Module to generate the pre-delays in this circuit.

One way to look at this circuit is that the Static Delays put four echos into the Diffuser Delay chain. Each Diffuser Delay then adds its own delay with feedback. That vastly increases the number of echos. When the delay times are very short the effect is like early reflections, while longer delay times emulate the reverb tail. A combination of delay times yields a fairly realistic room ambience.

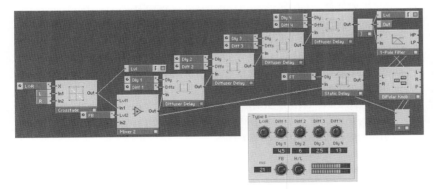

The Type II delay dispenses with the Static Delay Structure, stacks four Diffuser Delay Modules in series and adds a filtered feedback circuit to the whole process. The *FB* knob controls the amount of feedback and *ms* numerical controls the feedback delay time. The *H/L* knob is a bipolar knob with the left half controlling highpass cutoff and the right half controlling lowpass cutoff. The knob position also controls which filter is in effect. The Type II reverb is better for larger hall effects because of the compounding effect of the four delay lines.

It should be noted that both reverbs are monaural. The left and right input channels are mixed before being sent to the reverb units and the reverb units monaural output is then mixed back into both channels of the stereo output in an amount controlled by the *Wet/Dry* knob. A true stereo version of the Type II reverb is also provided (not connected in the Ensemble). Its control panel is identical, but a slight random variation in the four delay time settings for the right and left channels is introduced for more realistic stereo imaging. You'll also find both Instruments in the Instruments folder on the WIZOO CD.

MegaFX

▶ You'll find the MegaFX Ensemble in the Effects folder inside the Ensembles folder on the WIZOO CD.

The MegaFX Ensemble is a combination of effects we've seen before, configured in series and with on/off switches added to save CPU when some effects aren't needed. If you switch everything on, it can be quite a CPU hog and may only be usable at lower sampling rates.

The first effect in the series is a four-tap delay (see "Multi-tap Delay Lines" on page 187) with separate cross-feedback controls for each tap. The tap times can be quantized to note increments (quarter thru 1/64). The *Q-Beat* numerical selects the division of the beat (use zero for unquantized). The *L<f>R* knobs control the feedback amount to the left or right channels—which depends on the knob position.

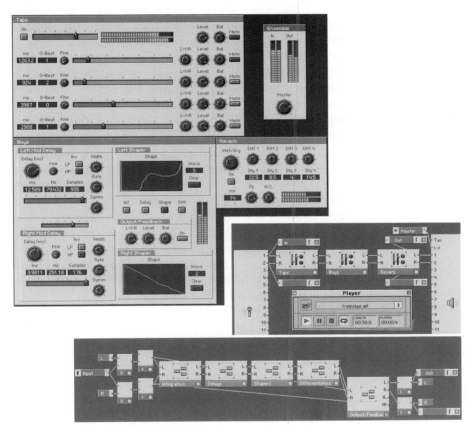

The next effect in the chain is the Instrument called Boyz, so named because it loosely resembles the Ohm Force plug-in, OhmBoyz. It starts with an Intergator filter, which provides a frequency-dependent boost to the low end (see "FTC: UnFilters" on page 178). The next stage is a feedback delay line with an LFO for modulating the delay amount (see "Phase Cancellation with Short Delays" on page 183). That is fol-

⊚ **58** MegaFx

lowed by a waveshaper that allows you to draw in your own waveshaping waveforms (see "The Shape of Things" on page 180). The last stage is a Differentiator filter, which provides a frequency-dependent boost to the high end. The Output/Feedback section allows you to feed either the left channel back to the right input or vice versa. Feedback is controlled by a bipolar knob as in the four-tap delay and the *On* button can be used to toggle feedback on and off. Finally, there are output-level and stereo-balance controls. Notice that each of the effects in the Boyz chain can be turned on and off independently.

The final stage is a stereo reverb with highpass or lowpass filtered feedback (see "Reverberation" on page 191). In fact, the entire effects chain is true stereo—there is separate effects processing for the left and right channels. The meters in each stage show that stage's output, while the meters in the Ensemble Control Panel show the overall input and output.

The MegaFX Ensemble is wired to process either audio input to Reaktor via the Ensemble's Audio Input Module or to process the playback of Reaktor's Audio File Player. Alternately, you could take any or all of the effects in the chain and use them in your own Structures. They are all provided as Instruments in the Instruments folder on the WIZOO CD.

7 Handy Gadgets & Tricks

In this chapter we'll provide some useful building blocks for enhancing your own or others' Ensembles. This is a rather eclectic collection and by no means comprehensive. You'll find Instruments and Macros for many more tasks in the Reaktor factory library and the Reaktor Users' library on Native Instruments' Web site: www.nativeinstruments.de

▶ You'll find Ensembles containing many of the gadgets in this section in the Gadgets folder inside the Ensembles folder on the WIZOO CD. You'll also find most of the gadgets as Macros in the Macros folder on the WIZOO CD.

Radio Buttons

Radio buttons get their name from the old style push-button radios where pushing one button on forces the other buttons off. Reaktor's Audio and Event Switches (Panels sub-menu of the Modules menu) operate this way—allowing only one input to pass to the switch's output. For occasions when you want to switch between more complex routing schemes, you can use this technique.

Radio Buttons Control Panel and simplified Structure for two radio buttons.

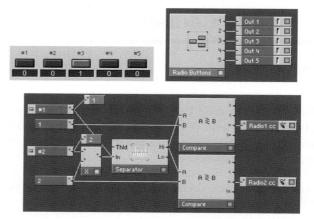

The Radio Buttons Macro has one output for each button. (Any number of buttons is possible—the Macro on the WIZOO CD contains five and the Structure in the illustration here shows the circuitry for two, which is the simplest case.) The outputs are wired directly to the numerical displays, which show value 1 when the button above is on and 0 when the button is off. Wiring these outputs to one input of an Event or Audio Mult 2 Module instead will cause the output of the Mult 2 Module to be either 0 or the value at the other input. For audio signals the effect is to pass or block the signal.

The rest of the Radio Button Structure is devoted to turning the other buttons off when any button is turned on. MIDI Controller Out Modules are used to remote control the buttons. (See illustration for the Properties set-up for each Button and MIDI Controller Out Module.) When a button is turned on, its value (which is one for each of the buttons) is multiplied by the button number. The output (i. e. the button number) is passed to a separate Compare Module for each MIDI Controller Out Module. The constants representing the button numbers are also wired to the other inputs of the Compare Modules, so that the = output of the Compare Module is 1 (a match) if its corresponding button is on and 0 (no match) if it is off. The MIDI Controller Out Modules therefore turn the non-matching buttons off. The purpose of the Separator Module is to only allow button-on Events to pass to the Compare Modules.

MIDI Controller Out and Button Properties. Note that the Controller numbers match, the Button's MIDI Remote is turned on and both Ranges are 0 to 1. The Button is in Toggle mode. The Instrument containing the Macro must also have Internal MIDI Routing turned on.

For an example of Radio Buttons in action have a look at the Ensemble named "Radio 3OP" in the WIZOO Ensembles folder. This is a three operator FM synth with radio buttons to choose from among five algorithms. (See "FM-1: Two-Operator FM Synth" on page 120.) The algorithms are symbolized by the arrays of three LEDs, which are also turned on when their algorithm is in use. (The LED arrangement for algorithm 4 is a bit obscure. That algorithm is an FM loop—1 to 2 to 3 to 1—with the output coming from operator 3.)

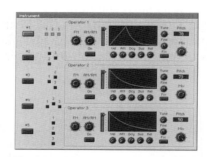

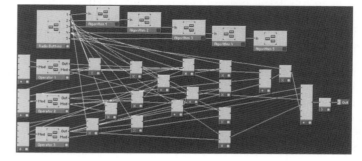

Radio 3OP Control Panel and Structure windows. The radio buttons along the left select the algorithms symbolized by the LEDs and light the LEDs of the active algorithm.

The Macros along the top of the Structure contain the LEDs and the Audio Mult 2 Modules below them set up the algorithms. The radio buttons are wired to the top input of each Audio Mult 2 Module to pass or block the signal at its other input.

Control Randomizer

This is for occasions when you want to randomize the settings of Reaktor Control Panel elements. Of course, you can also send random values directly to Module inputs, but these are not saved in Snapshots and you don't get to watch the controls dance around. The most obvious application of this technique is to create new sounds or sequences by scrambling some or all control settings, but randomization can also be used as a real-time sound effect. (See "NewsCool" on page 71 for an example.)

The Random 1 Macro
is the most economical way to randomize
a Control Panel element.

The most efficient (no bells and whistles) way to randomize a Reaktor Control Panel element is shown in the Random 1 Macro. Events arriving at the *In* input are set to zero (using the Event Mult 2 Module with one input unconnected). A constant is added using the Constant Module labeled "Center".

► The event arriving at the Randomize Module's In input is, therefore, equal to the constant.

The Module labeled "+/− Rnd" is also a Constant, which determines the maximum random deviation applied by the Randomize Module. The output of the Randomize Module is sent to the MIDI Controller Out Module.

To use the Random 1 Macro, import it into any Instrument and set the MIDI Controller Out Module to the same MIDI Controller number as the Control Panel element to be randomized. Cable the triggering device (e. g. a Button Module) into the Macro's *In* input. Ensure that the target Control Panel element has MIDI Remote turned on and that the Instrument has Internal MIDI Routing turned on.

The Random 4 Macro (left) contains four randomizers and replaces the constants in Random 1 by an xy Module. Display meters showing the random value are also added.
The Random 16 Instrument (right) combines four Random 4 Macros with a Button Module to gate all four.

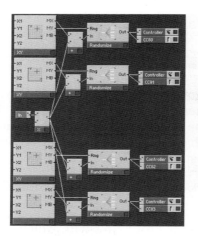

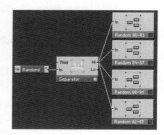

The Random 4 Macro combines four randomizers with xy Modules for setting the center and range of each. Meters are also added to display the current random values. Button and Separator Modules are used to gate the randomizers.

▶ The Separator ensures that the values change only when the button is pressed (i. e. not also when it is released.

Alternately, you could use a sequencer or lfo to gate the Random 4 Macros.

The Random 16 Instrument uses a button to gate four Random 4 Macros set up for midi Controllers 80 through 95. Of course, you can change the midi Controller numbers as needed. To use the Random 16 Instrument, make sure both its and the target Instrument's Internal midi Routing properties are turned on, assign both Instruments to the same midi channel and set up remote control of the target Instrument's Control Panel elements that you want randomized to match the midi Controller Out Module settings in Random 16.

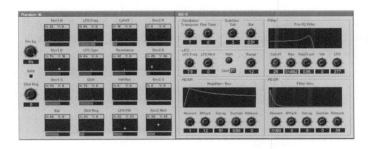

The Random BS-5 Ensemble applies the Random 16 Instrument to the BS-5 synthesizer Instrument.

In the Gadgets folder, you'll also find a version of Random 16 used with the BS-5 synthesizer (see "BS-5: LFO and Sample-and-Hold" on page 94). In this version of Random 16, the center and range knobs have been replaced by XY Modules—horizontal position sets the center and vertical position sets the range. Reaktor's internal sequencer clock is used to both trigger the random changes and the BS-5's envelopes. A separate, quantized randomizer is used for overall pitch to produce a sample-and-hold effect.

Modulation Matrix

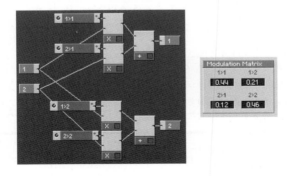

2 × 2 Modulation Matrix Macro Structure (left) and its Control Panel (right)

In "FM-2: Five-Operator Matrix-FM Synth" on page 125 we used a five-by-five modulation matrix to control the modulation routings among five FM operators. This two-by-two version shows how it was done. You'll find both this and the five-by-five version in the Macros folder on the WIZOO CD.

Each audio input is multiplied by a "scaling factor" set by one of the numericals in the Control Panel. The scaled inputs are then added and sent to the modulation output.

▶ You can create numerical controls in Reaktor by turning any control's "Picture" property off in the Properties' Appearance section.

Output Switch

Output Switch Macro Structure.

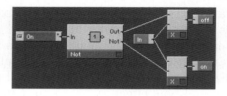

Reaktor contains a number of Modules dedicated to routing event and audio signals. These are shown in the table below:

Module	Inputs	Outputs	Remote
Panel: Audio Switch (A)	1, 2, 3, 4, 5, 6, 8	1	no
Panel: Audio Switch (A)	2 pair	2	no
Panel: Event Switch (E)	1, 2, 3, 4, 5, 6, 8	1	no
Mixer: Scanner (A)	8	1	yes
Audio Mod: Relay (A)	1, 2	1	yes
Event Proc: Router	1, 2	1	yes
Event Proc: Router	1	16	yes

The one option that is missing is a simple way to switch one input between two outputs. As the illustration indicates, this is quite easy to do. The *On* switch toggles between values 0 (off) and 1 (on). The *Out* output of the Not Module always has the opposite value while the *Not* output always has the switch value. Multiplying the input by the Not Module outputs does the trick. Audio and event versions of this Macro are provided in the Macros folder on the WIZOO CD.

Automated Knob

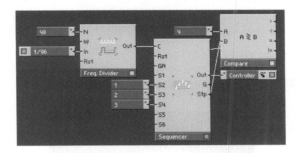

Macro Structure for automating a knob synchronized to Reaktor's internal clock.

This Macro can be used to make a Control Panel knob or slider cycle through several positions in synchronization with Reaktor's internal clock.

▶ Reaktor's sequencer transport must be running for this Macro to work.

The ¹⁄₉₆ Module sends out 96 triggers per beat at the tempo (BPM) setting in the Ensemble Toolbar. The Freq. Divider Module counts these triggers and lets one pass when the count reaches the value at its *N* input. In the example, that value is 48, so the Freq. Divider Module sends out one trigger per half-beat.

The triggers from the Freq. Divider Module step the Sequencer Module through its sequence and its output value corresponds to the input for the current step. In the example, the values for the steps *S1*, *S2*, *S3* and *S4* are zero through four, respectively. The Controller Module outputs these values as MIDI Controller messages, which automate any Control Panel element set to respond to the same MIDI Controller number.

▶ The Instrument containing the Macro must have Internal MIDI Routing turned on for that to work.

The function of the Compare Module is to reset the Sequencer Module to step zero after four steps. It compares the current step number sent from the Sequencer Module *Stp* output to a constant value (4 in this case) and sends a value of one from its = output when they match.

BiPolar Knob

Macro Structure for a bipolar knob. The *R* output is active when the knob's value is positive (>0) and the *L* output is active, otherwise (≤0). The outputs are scaled by the positive part of the knob's value.

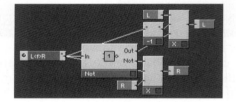

Use this Macro to control one parameter when the knob's value is negative and another when the knob's value is positive. The affected parameter is multiplied by the knob's absolute value (i. e. the positive part of its value) while the other parameter is held at zero. (For an example, see "Multi-tap Delay Lines" on page 187.)

   The Not Module sends a one from its *Out* output when the knob's value is less than or equal to zero and sends a zero from that output otherwise. The Not Module sends the complimentary logical value from its *Not* output. The Mult 3 Modules multiply the Not Module's outputs by the *L* and *R* inputs and the knob values. (Note that the knob value is inverted for the *L* output, which is active when the knob's value is negative.)

▶ There's no reason why you have to restrict this action to knobs—it works equally well with sliders or internally generated signals—such as an LFO's output (see "Comparitor" below).

Comparitor

 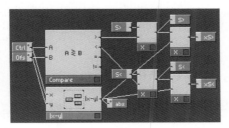

Macro Structure for the bipolar control processor—an expanded version of the BiPolar Knob Macro.

This Macro generalizes the BiPolar Knob Macro, by comparing two event signals and routing two audio signals according to which event is larger:

♦ *S<*, *S>* inputs: audio inputs for the signals to be routed during the < and > parts of the comparison. If the *Ctrl* input is less than or equal to the *Ofs* input then the *S<* and *xS<* inputs are routed to the *S<* and *xS<* outputs. Otherwise, the *S>* and *xS>* inputs are routed to the *S>* and *xS>* outputs.

♦ *Ctrl* input: event input for the left half of the comparison.

♦ *Ofs* input: event input for the right half of the comparison.

♦ *S<*, *S>* outputs: audio outputs for the unscaled input signal. *S<* will be the same as the *S<* input when *Ctrl* ≤ *Ofs* and will be zero otherwise. *S>* will be the same as the *S>* input when *Ctrl* > *Ofs* and will be zero otherwise.

If you add the *S<* and *S>* outputs, then the Comparitor is similar to a cross-switch. If you add the *xS<* and *S>x* outputs then the Comparitor is similar to a crossfade except that both sides fade to zero.

◆ *xS<*, *xS>* outputs: same as *S<* and *S>* outputs except scaled by the absolute difference of the compared values ($|Ctrl - Ofs|$).

◆ *abs* output: the absolute difference of the compared values ($|Ctrl - Ofs|$).

▶ Using an automated input for the *Ctrl* input such as an LFO, random generator or sequencer provides interesting signal routing possibilities.

Units and Conversions

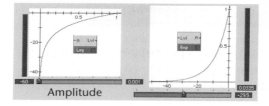

Amplitude

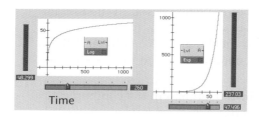

Time

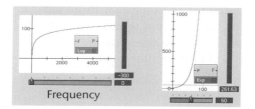

Frequency

Hz/ms/samples

BPM/ms/samples

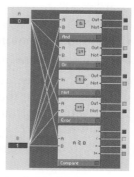

Logic Modules

Reaktor uses linear scaling for some of its Module inputs and logarithmic/exponential scaling for others. The folks at Native Instruments have endeavored to make the most logical choice in each case, but you will inevitably come across a situation when you want the option they haven't implemented. Being one step ahead of us, as usual, they have provided converter Modules for just that purpose. They are located in the Shaper sub-menu. The Exp Modules are available in both event and audio flavors, but the Log Modules are only available as event Modules.

The three types of inputs where this arises are:

◆ Amplitude (usual range: zero to one) versus decibels in dB below unity gain (usual range: −60 to zero).

▶ 0dB corresponds to an amplitude of 1 and a change of ±20dB corresponds to multiplying or dividing the amplitude by 10.

◆ Time measured in milliseconds versus time measured logarithmically in $^{dB}/_{ms}$.

▶ $0^{dB}/_{ms} = 1ms$, $20^{dB}/_{ms} = 10ms$, $40^{dB}/_{ms} = 100ms$, etc.

◆ Frequency measured in Hertz versus pitch measured in MIDI Note numbers.

▶ Note 69 corresponds to 440Hz and a change of ±12 notes corresponds to multiplying or dividing the frequency by 2.

The same conversion Modules are used for amplitude and time conversion whereas frequency has its own conversion Module. Each of the conversion processes is illustrated by an Instrument in the Conversion Ensemble with a graphic of the shaping curve, a horizontal slider for the input value (the value to be converted) and a vertical meter for the output value. The graph also shows the correct Module to use for the conversion. The Instruments are provided separately in the Instruments folder on the WIZOO CD for easy reference while working on your own Ensembles.

Probably the most familiar example to illustrate the difference between linear and exponential scaling is the relation between pitch as represented by MIDI Note numbers (where a rise of one octave corresponds to adding 12) and frequency as measured in Hertz (where a rise of one octave corresponds to multiplying by 2). The relation between an additive scale (e.g. MIDI Note numbers) and a multiplicative scale (e.g. frequency) is called "exponential". Therefore, when you want to use MIDI Note numbers to set a Module's F input, you use the Event Expon. (F) or Audio Expon. (F) Module.

The labels on most Module's inputs indicate which kind of unit is expected. For example, F inputs are linear and expect frequency values in Hz whereas P inputs are exponential and expect MIDI Note numbers. A inputs expect linear amplitude, but Lvl inputs expect logarithmic dB values. Most envelope Module inputs expect logarithmic time values in dB/ms, however, they are usually labeled to indicate the parameter they control (e.g. A for attack, H for hold, etc.)

▶ For amplitude/level and frequency/pitch, the trick to remembering which Modules to use is to match up the conversion Module's output label with the destination Module's input label. For time conversion, you'll almost always want the Log(A) Module, which converts milliseconds to dB/ms—the typical input for envelope time-parameters.

All Reaktor Control Panel controls are linear—that just means that moving the control the same distance always produces the same change in value regardless of where on the control the movement occurs. The event shaper Modules are handy in cases where that is not convenient. For example, you might want delay-time settings to change slowly at first and more quickly later as you move a control from the bottom to the top of its range. Or, you might want an LFO's frequency to change rapidly at first and more slowly later. From the graphs in the illustration, you can see that the exponential shapers (labeled "Exp") will do the first job and the logarithmic shapers (labeled "Log") will do the second.

▶ This technique is used for the delay-time settings in the Delays Ensemble on page 183.

Keep in mind that you'll need to adjust the value ranges of the controls to achieve the desired output range.

The Conversion Ensemble also contains three handy cal-culators. One calculates the time and number of samples (at a 44,100Hz sampling rate) for quarter-notes, 1⁄16-notes and 1⁄16-note triplets. Another converts frequency in Hertz to the time and number of samples (again at 44,100) for one cycle.

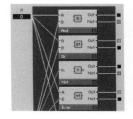

▶ That calculator is built into the delay-time controls of the Delays Ensemble on page 183.

A third illustrates the action of Reaktor's five Logic Modules: And, Or, Not, xor and Compare. These convert numbers or pairs of numbers into the logical values zero (false) and one (true). The logic calculator provides numericals for setting the inputs to the logic Modules and LEDs for displaying their outputs. The LED is on when the corresponding output value is one (true).

Math Gadgets

Macros for making
some useful calcula-
tions.

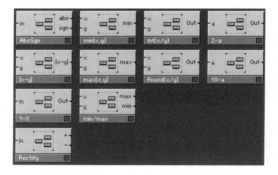

No matter how much you try to avoid it, sooner or later
you're going to have to do some basic calculations in Reaktor
for which there are no specific Modules. Here are some Macros to get you started:

◆ *AbsSgn:* calculates the absolute value (i. e. the positive
part or quantity) and the sign (i. e. +1 or −1) of the input
value.

◆ *|x −y|:* calculates the absolute difference between two
numbers. That is x − y if x is bigger than y and y − x otherwise.

◆ *1−X:* subtracts the incoming value from 1. This is a useful
for creating crossfades when the input ranges from zero
to one.

◆ *Rectify:* when the input is positive it is passed to the + output and when it is negative its positive part (i. e. absolute
value) is passed to the − output. That is like an event rectifier with separate outputs for the positive and negative
side.

▶ The Abs output of AbsSgn is like an event rectifier with one output.

◆ *Min(x,y):* calculates the minimum of its two inputs.

- *Max(x,y):* calculates the maximum of its two inputs.
- *Min/Max:* calculates both the minimum and maximum of its two inputs.
- *Int(x/y):* calculates the integer part of x/y. That is the smallest integer not greater than x/y.
- *Round(x/y):* rounds x/y to the closest integer.
- *2^a:* calculates the ath power of 2.
- *10^a:* calculates the ath power of 10.

You'll find each of these Macros separately in in the Macros folder on the WIZOO CD. You also find an Instrument containing all of them in in the Instruments folder on the WIZOO CD.

Closest Harmonic

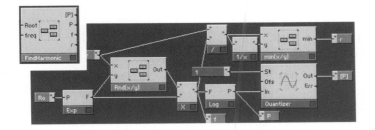

Macro for finding the harmonic of a pitch that is closest to another frequency.

The term harmonic refers to integer multiples of a given frequency. (Additive synthesis—see "Add-1: Additive Synthesis" on page 116—creates complex waveforms by adding individual harmonics.) The purpose of this Macro is to calculate the frequency of the harmonic of one frequency that is closest to another frequency. The "root" frequency should be input as a note number and the target frequency should be input in Hertz. There are outputs for the rounded *[P]* and un-rounded *P* note number of the harmonic as well as the frequency of the root note *f* and the ratio of the two frequencies *r*.

Appendix

Frequently Asked Questions

Here are answers to some of the more common questions from Reaktor users. Needless to say, we've purposely left out your most pressing question.

How can I get the latest Reaktor update.

Registered Reaktor users can download the latest updates from the Native Instruments Web site: www.nativeinstruments.de

Sometimes I see red X's at some Module inputs and everything stops working.

In polyphonic Instruments (i. e. Instruments with voice settings higher than one), Reaktor must keep separate calculations going for each of the voices. You can see this in the wires when you mouse over them with Hints turned on. Before Reaktor can play the sounds it is calculating, it must combine them into a single audio signal. The Audio Voice Combiner Module is provided for that purpose. The red X appears when you wire an uncombined output to an input of a mono Module. (Most Modules have a mono checkbox in their Properties window.) The solution here is to either turn the receiving Module's mono property off or use an Audio Voice Combiner Module before the input.

Another case where this occurs is with the inputs and outputs to Instruments you construct. All Instrument inputs only accept mono or voice-combined signals. For that reason, it is always a good idea to use an Audio Voice Combiner Module before any Instrument output, even if the Instrument is monophonic.

For more details see "Voices, Channels and Outputs" on page 21 and "Polyphony and the Dread Red X" on page 107.

Sometimes I get audible clicks when I use audio switches or change Snapshots.

When you change an audio switch position, Reaktor "recalculates" the entire Instrument behind the switch to de-activate Modules that have been taken out of the signal path and activate Modules that have been put into it. This process allows Reaktor to make the most efficient use of your CPU by not making needless calculations. The re-calculating process has become much more efficient in Reaktor 3 to minimize this problem.

In the case of Snapshots there may be two causes. The first is the changing of audio switches mentioned above and the second is abrupt changes in the nature of the audio signal as a result of the new Snapshot settings.

In both cases, the solution is to avoid making these changes when audio is playing.

If my audio card and drivers use a 44,100 Hertz sampling rate, is there any point in using higher sample rate settings in Reaktor?

Yes. Reaktor does all its internal calculations at the higher rate and that can have audible results (see Snapshot 13 of the Delays Ensemble in "Phase Cancellation with Short Delays" on page 183).

What does it mean when the little yellow lights on the Module icons turn gray.

The yellow light indicates that a Reaktor element (i. e. a Module, Macro or Instrument) is active. It turns gray when the element is taken out of the signal path. This may happen when an audio switch is changed from one position to another, for example. It can also happen if you make wiring changes that break the path from the element to the audio output.

Is Reaktor mono, poly or multi?

Yes.

Reaktor can record and play monaural or stereo audio files. Its audio output can have up to 16 audio channels depending on your sound card and drivers.

Reaktor processing within Instruments can be monophonic (one voice) or polyphonic (multiple voices, processed separately). Audio signals entering and leaving Instruments, must be "voice-combined"—i. e. the separate voices are combined into a single audio signal.

You can create multi-timbral Reaktor Ensembles by assigning different Instruments within the Ensemble to different MIDI Channels. You can also assign different Instruments to different audio outputs. But, you can only load one Ensemble at a time into Reaktor during stand-alone operation.

How can I tell how much CPU an Instrument or Macro is using?

Select Measure CPU Usage from Reaktor's System menu while audio is enabled and each Module's usage will be displayed. (Audio is disabled during this mode of operation.)

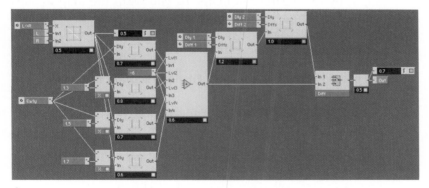

↑ CPU Usage is indicated for each Structure element in the black field at the bottom.

How do I set the frequency to get an LFO to cycle in ⅛-notes?

Short answer: BPM/30.

Long answer: To sync the LFO to ⅛-notes, you need to set its frequency to the number of ⅛-notes per second. Start with the tempo in beats-per-minute (BPM) and divide it into 60. That gives you the number of seconds for one beat. Divide that by two because there are two ⅛-notes in a beat. You now have the number of seconds for an ⅛-note. Divide that into one (use the Event 1/X Module) to find the number of ⅛-notes per second (i. e. the LFO frequency).

General answer: Notes-per-beat × BPM/60.

How do I set a samplers loop-length to play one beat of a sample-loop.

First you need to know two things: the number of beats in the sample-loop and the length of the sample-loop in milliseconds. You'll have to figure the first out by listening, but many of Reaktor's sampler Modules have an output labeled *Lng* that will tell you the sample's length in milliseconds. Now, to find the loop-length for one beat, divide the total length by the number of beats. (If you want the loop to start somewhere other than the first beat, multiply the milliseconds-per-beat calculation by the desired starting beat and use that to set the loop-start.)

I've played with all the factory Ensembles and I'm bored. Where can I get more?

There's an active library of user Ensembles at the Native Instruments Web site: www.nativeinstruments.de

Why do some Ensembles have two wires connected to the same Module input?

When two or more wires are connected to the same event input, the value at that input will be from the wire whose value changed last. (You can not connect two wires to an audio input.) That might be useful, for example, if you want to gate a Module with both an on-screen button and a MIDI gate.

Sometimes I see inputs to a Mult. Module left unconnected. Doesn't that mean the output is always zero?

Yes and that can be useful for a number of reasons. One example is to activate a Module by connecting it to an audio output. The connection will have no effect on the audio signal, but will make the Module active.

CD-ROM Contents

Data Section

The Data Section contains all the Reaktor Ensembles and Instruments described in the book plus a Native Instruments Demo Folder containing a fully functional (save disabled) Reaktor demo allowing every reader to try out the examples, even before they buy Reaktor.

Audio Section

The audio section features 57 examples designed to accompany the book. The following table lists the examples and the pages that refer to them.

The first audio track on the CD is a data set-up track that does not contain any audio. That will show up as Track 1 on most commercial CD players, and we have started our numbering of the audio examples accordingly—the first example is labeled Track 2. If you play the audio CD in your computer's CD-ROM drive, the data set-up track may not show up as an audio track at all. In that case, numbers in the text are off by 1—e.g. select Track 1 when the text refers to Track 2, etc.

Glossary

ADSR	Attack, Decay, Sustain, Release: typical envelope used in classic analog synthesizers.
AIFF	Audio Interchange File Format. A widely used format for audio files invented by Apple Computer. Reaktor samplers and recorders can load audio files in AIFF or WAVE format.
Amplifier	A device which controls the level of a signal.
Amplitude	Amplitude is a term used to describe the amount of a signal. It can relate to volume in an audio signal or the amount of voltage in an electrical signal.
Audio input	Module input to which you can connect audio signals (⇨ Event input). Audio signals are processed at a Reaktor's audio sampling rate, which can be as low as 22,050 Hertz or as high as 132,300 Hertz.
Chorus	A voice doubling effect created by layering two identical sounds with a delay and slightly modulating the frequency of one or both of the sounds to give the illusion of multiple voices.
Clock	A steady, periodic pulse typically used to control the timing of a sequencer's steps.
Cutoff	The frequency at which the signal passing through a low- or highpass filter is attenuated by 3dB.
Decibel (dB)	A logarithmic measure of the ratio of two values. An increase of 3dB represents a doubling in value and an increase of 10dB represents multiplication by 10. It is important to remember that dB is a measure of change, not quantity. However, it can be used as a measure of quantity if the denominator in the ratio is a constant. Reaktor envelopes, for example, measure time in dB referenced to 1 millisecond (e. g. $^{dB}\!/_{ms}$).
DSP	Digital Signal Processing: modifying some aspect of an audio signal that has been created digitally (i. e. by digital computation) or converted into digital information (i. e. using an analog-to-digital converter).
Ensemble	Reaktor's highest level structure. Reaktor files are called Ensembles. There is always one and only one Ensemble running in Reaktor at a time.
Envelope	The shape of a slow, one-time variation in some aspect of an audio signal path—most commonly the amplitude or filter cutoff frequency. (⇨ ADSR)
Event input	Module input to which you can connect control signals (⇨ Audio input). Control signals are processed at a much lower sampling rate than audio signals and therefore use much less CPU time.

Event Merge	Reaktor Module for merging consecutive events of the same value. An Event Merge Module might be used to prevent multiple triggers, for example.
Flanging	The process of summing a signal with a delayed copy of itself in which the amount of delay is varied over time (usually with an LFO). The name derives from the original mechanical means for producing this effect using tape recorders and human fingers on the flanges of the tape reels. (⇨Phasing)
FM	Frequency modulation. The process of modulating the frequency of an audio oscillator by an audio-rate signal (typically from another audio oscillator).
Frequency	The rate of a periodically repeating process—e. g. oscillation. Frequency is usually measured in Hertz (cycles-per-second). The period of oscillation in seconds—i. e. the time for one cycle—is the reciprocal of the frequency ($\frac{1}{f}$). Generally the period in milliseconds ($\frac{1000}{f}$) is more useful.
Gate	A control signal that rises instantly to a specified value (usually one) and is held there for a length of time. Gate signals are usually generated by some mechanical device (e. g. a MIDI keyboard), an on-screen button or a periodic generator like a clock-oscillator. In Reaktor, when MIDI Note messages are used for gate signals, the MIDI Note-on Velocity can be used to scale the Gate value.
Hard-Sync	A process in which one oscillator's wave form is forced to re-start at a rate determined by another oscillator.
Instrument	Reaktor's highest structural element. ⇨Ensembles are usually made up of one or more Instruments. Instruments can be monophonic or polyphonic and can have multiple audio inputs and outputs. Instruments have their own MIDI Channel assignment and their ownSnapshots. Instruments can be saved to disk for use in other Ensembles.
Key Scaling	Scaling the value of some parameter (e. g. filter cutoff frequency) by MIDI Note numbers.
LFO	Low Frequency Oscillator. An oscillator used for generating control signals whose rate of oscillation is below the audio range (typically, between zero and 30 Hertz).
Macro	Reaktor's middle level of organization. Macros are containers for collecting other Macros and Modules in order to simplify the structure inside Reaktor Instruments. Macros can be saved to disk for use in other Ensembles.

Map	A collection of individual audio files mapped across the MIDI Note range. Most Reaktor sampler Modules will load and save map files as well as loading individual audio files in WAVE or AIFF format. Reaktor can also convert AKAI format files into Reaktor map files.
MIDI	Acronym for Musical Instrument Digital Interface. MIDI enables synthesizers, sequencers, computers, rhythm machines, etc. to be interconnected through a standard interface and exchange notes controllers, clock and sounds. MIDI dictates a uniform data format and connector standard for all manufacturers.
MIDI Controller	A mechanical device (keyboard, wheel, joystick, etc.) that sends MIDI Controller messages.
Module	Reaktor's most basic building block. Modules are part of the Reaktor program and can not be modified. They perform a single task and have audio and control inputs and outputs appropriate to that task.
Monaural (Mono)	Limiting an Instrument or Ensemble to one audio output.
Monophonic (Mono)	Limiting an Instrument or Ensemble to one-voice.
Multi-timbral	The ability to produce different sounds (timbres) in response to MIDI Notes on different MIDI Channels. (A singer is monophonic, a piano is polyphonic and an orchestra is multi-timbral.)
Noise	A randomly generated audio signal. The audio characteristic of "white" noise is that it contains no frequency information. Put another way, a long-term frequency analysis of the signal will show all frequencies present at equal amplitudes. Filtering white noise results in "colored" noise (referred to as pink, red, etc.).
Nyquist frequency	The highest frequency sine wave that can, theoretically, be reproduced at a given sampling rate. It is one-half the sampling rate.
Oscillator	An analog circuit or digital calculation that generates a periodically repeating pattern.
Overdrive	Distortion produced by overloading a vacuum tube circuit. Digitally this is usually simulated by some sort of clipping.
Panorama	Position of the audio signal in the stereo field.
Phasing	An effect similar to flanging (⇨ Flanging), in which phase shifted copies of a signal are mixed with itself with the amount of phase shift varied over time. The effect is less pronounced than flanging.
Pitch	A subjective measure of frequency perception. In the context if MIDI and Reaktor, pitch is measured by MIDI Note number. MIDI Note number 60 corresponds to Middle C and a frequency of 261.63Hz.

Polyphony	The number of voices an Instrument can produce. Different Reaktor Instruments within the same Ensemble can have different polyphonies. The special case of one-voice is called monophonic.
Portamento	Continuous gliding from one pitch to another, also referred to as glide.
Quantize	The restriction of an audio or control signal to equally spaced, discrete values (often integers).
Resonance	A frequency at which a filter exhibits a spectral peak.
Sample & Hold	A periodic sampling of a control or audio signal to produce discrete values held for equal periods of time. The classic application of this technique to generate a random sequence of notes at a fixed clock rate.
Sequencer	A construction that generates a series of pitches or control values at a regularly spaced time intervals (the clock rate).
Snapshot	Reaktor's version of a synthesizer preset. Snapshots apply to individual Reaktor Instruments. Individual Instrument Snapshots can be collected on the Ensemble level as Ensemble Snapshots.
Trigger	A momentary pulse typically used to start an envelope generator through its pattern. (⇨Gate).
Velocity	In the context of MIDI, the velocity is the speed at which a key on a MIDI keyboard travels, when pressed. In MIDI synthesizers that is often used to affect the signal's amplitude.
Voice Combiner	Reaktor Module for combining the individual voice calculations in a polyphonic Instrument into one audio signal. Any polyphonic Instrument should have one of these before each of its audio outputs.
WAVE	Microsoft's adaptation of the Electronic Arts Interchange File Format. Due to the ubiquity of the Windows platform, this is the most common format for audio files. Reaktor will import these as well as AIFF files into its sampler and recorder Modules.
Waveset	An audio file consisting of many single- or multi-cycle waveforms. In Oscil. Mode, Reaktor's samplers will play the individual waveforms like a digital oscillator.
Wire	Reaktor's term for the cables that connect its Modules together.

Index